RUDOLPH THE RED-NOSED REINDEER®

THE ISLAND OF MISFIT TOYS™

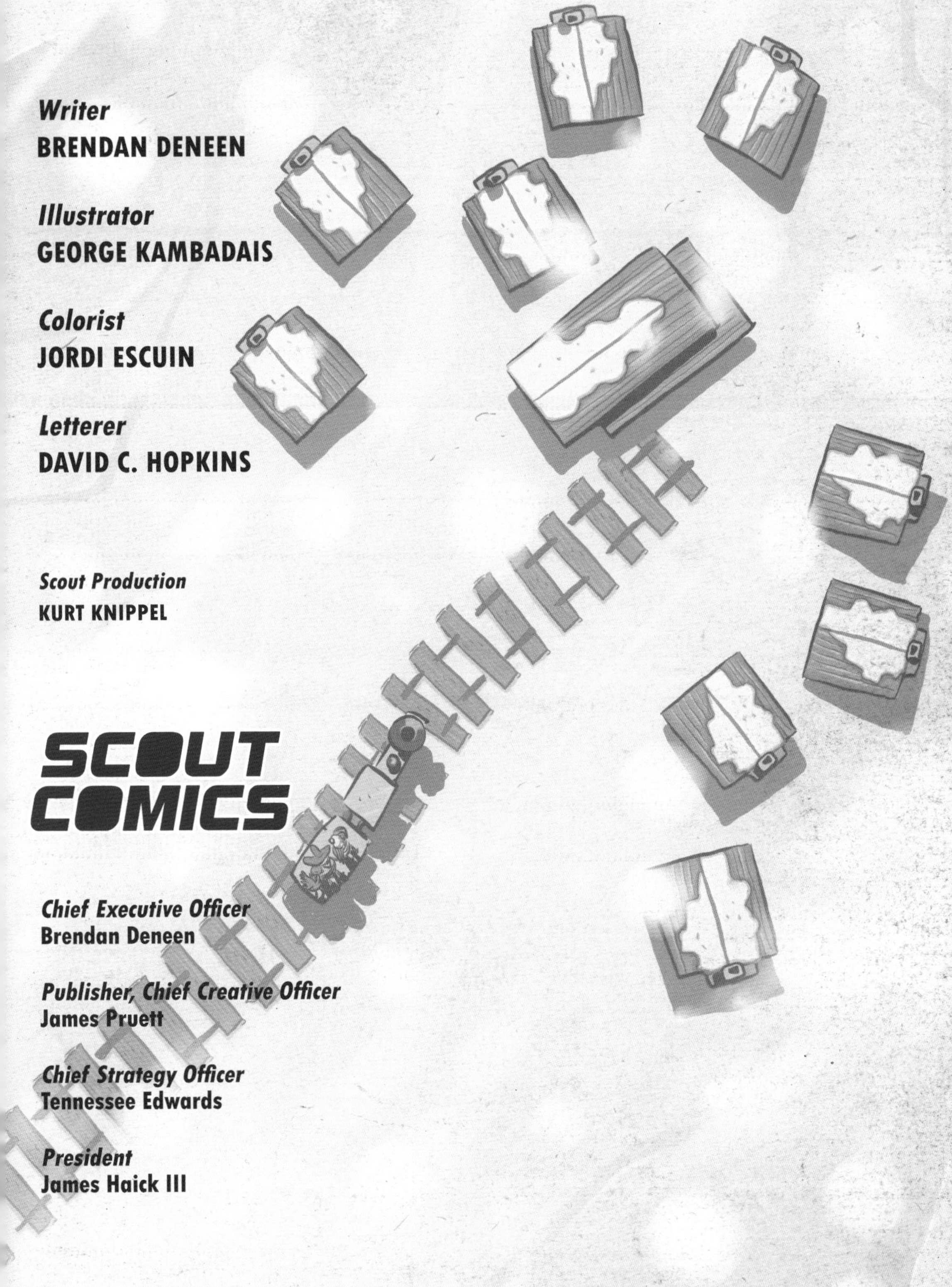

Writer
BRENDAN DENEEN

Illustrator
GEORGE KAMBADAIS

Colorist
JORDI ESCUIN

Letterer
DAVID C. HOPKINS

Scout Production
KURT KNIPPEL

SCOUT COMICS

Chief Executive Officer
Brendan Deneen

Publisher, Chief Creative Officer
James Pruett

Chief Strategy Officer
Tennessee Edwards

President
James Haick III

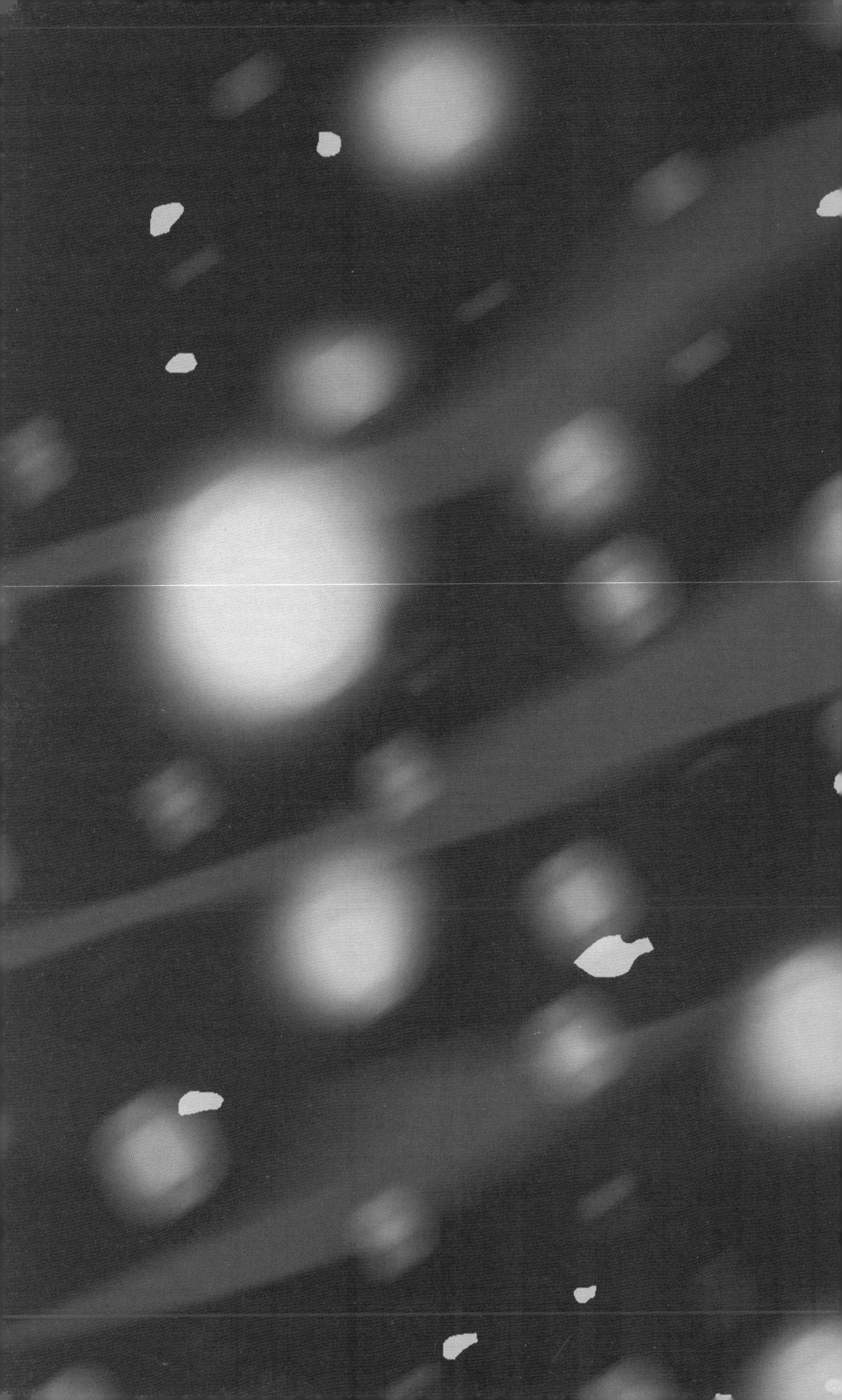

For Eloise and Charlotte, the best gifts I've ever received.
—B.D.

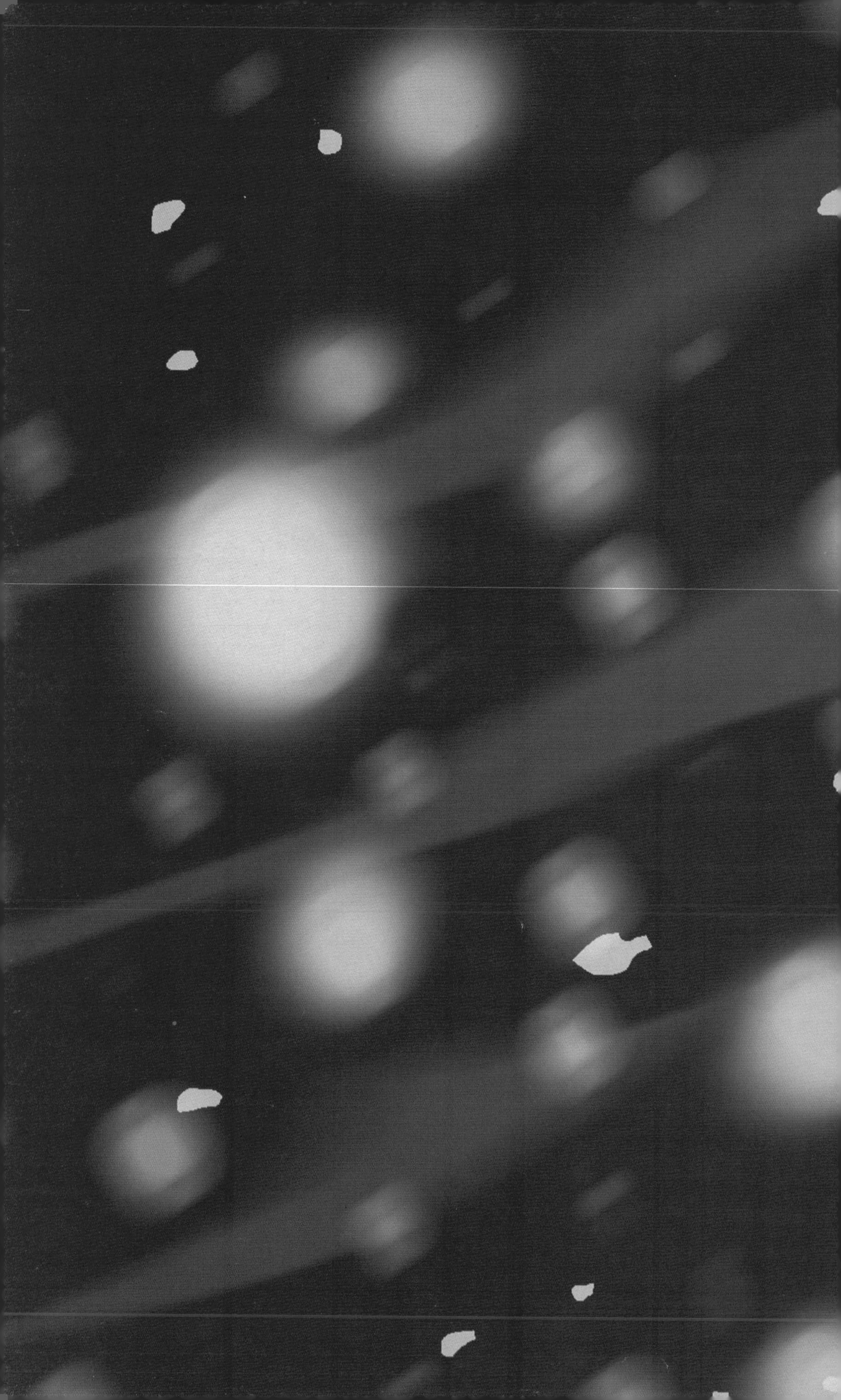

RUDOLPH THE RED-NOSED REINDEER®

THE ISLAND OF MISFIT TOYS™

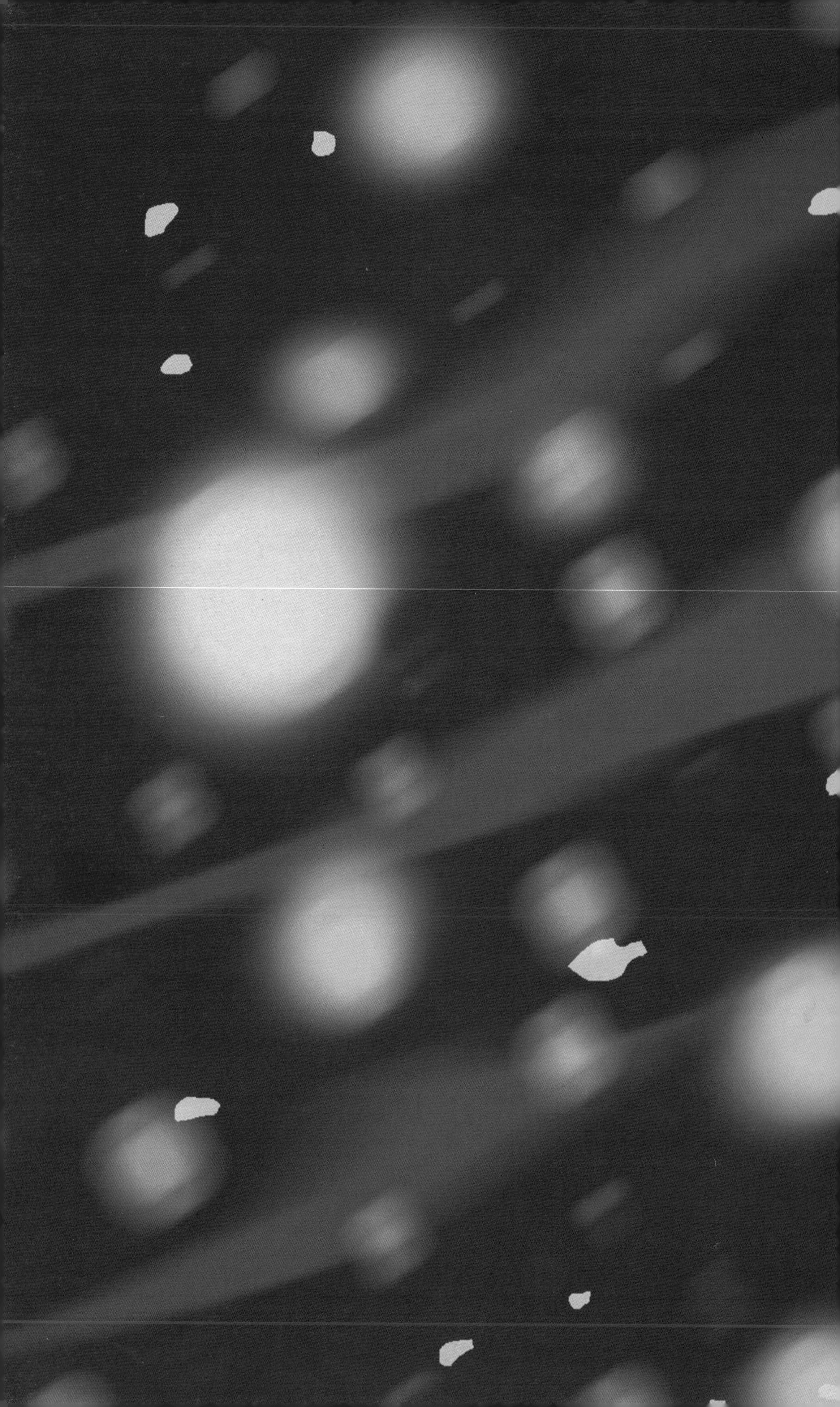

CHAPTER ONE

THE STORM

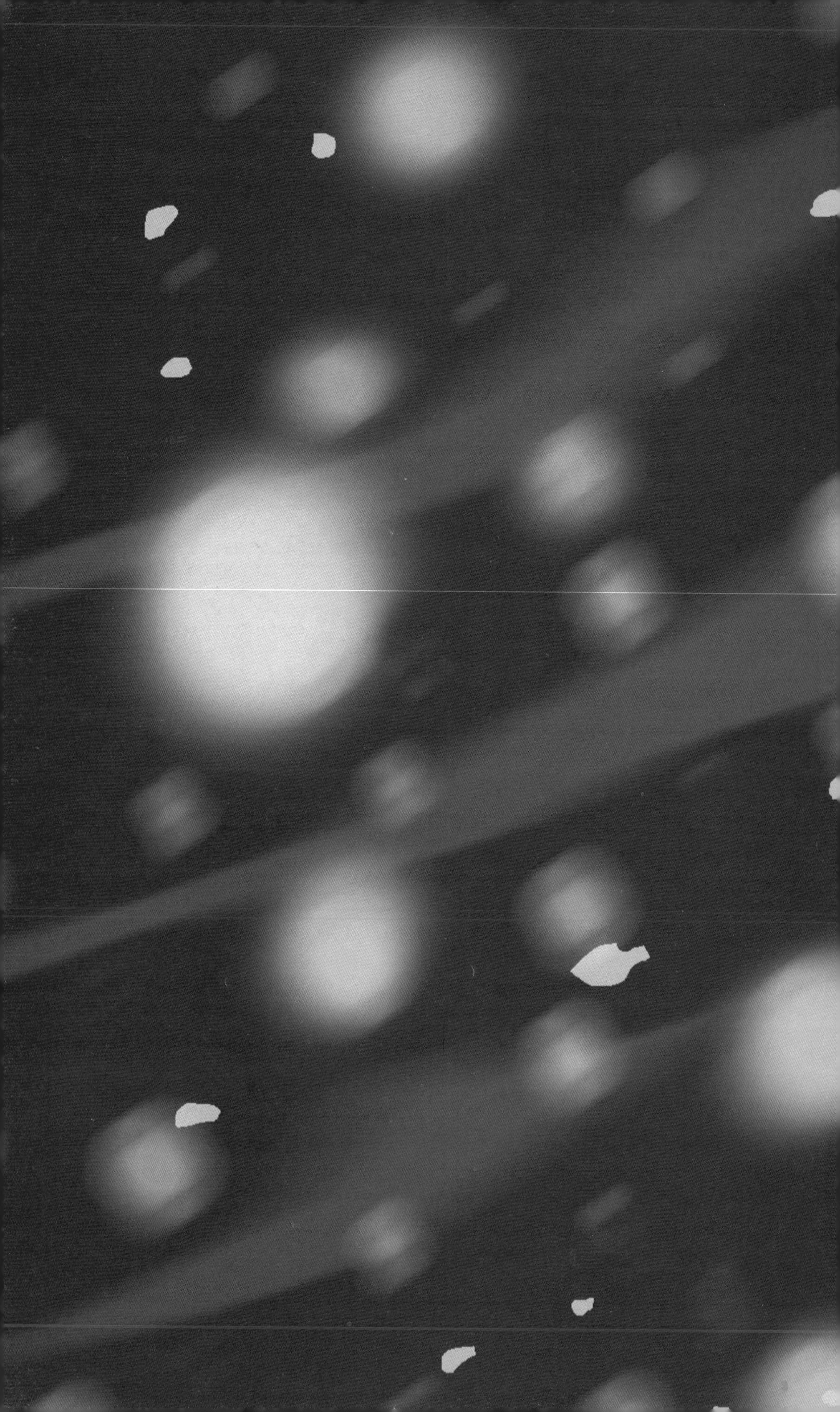

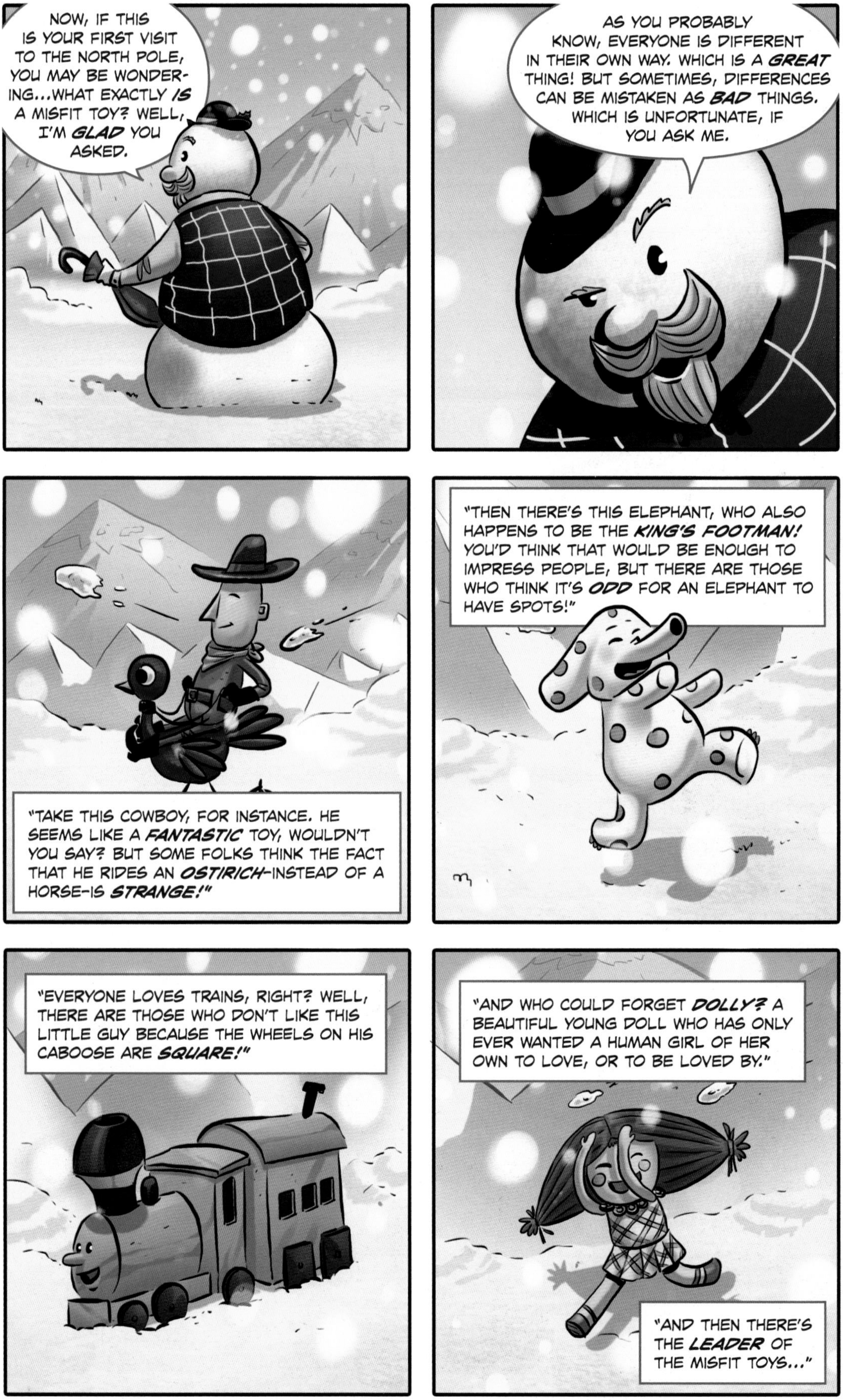
NOW, IF THIS IS YOUR FIRST VISIT TO THE NORTH POLE, YOU MAY BE WONDERING...WHAT EXACTLY *IS* A MISFIT TOY? WELL, I'M *GLAD* YOU ASKED.
AS YOU PROBABLY KNOW, EVERYONE IS DIFFERENT IN THEIR OWN WAY. WHICH IS A *GREAT* THING! BUT SOMETIMES, DIFFERENCES CAN BE MISTAKEN AS *BAD* THINGS. WHICH IS UNFORTUNATE, IF YOU ASK ME.
"TAKE THIS COWBOY, FOR INSTANCE. HE SEEMS LIKE A *FANTASTIC* TOY, WOULDN'T YOU SAY? BUT SOME FOLKS THINK THE FACT THAT HE RIDES AN *OSTIRICH*–INSTEAD OF A HORSE–IS *STRANGE!*"
"THEN THERE'S THIS ELEPHANT, WHO ALSO HAPPENS TO BE THE *KING'S FOOTMAN!* YOU'D THINK THAT WOULD BE ENOUGH TO IMPRESS PEOPLE, BUT THERE ARE THOSE WHO THINK IT'S *ODD* FOR AN ELEPHANT TO HAVE SPOTS!"
"EVERYONE LOVES TRAINS, RIGHT? WELL, THERE ARE THOSE WHO DON'T LIKE THIS LITTLE GUY BECAUSE THE WHEELS ON HIS CABOOSE ARE *SQUARE!*"
"AND WHO COULD FORGET *DOLLY?* A BEAUTIFUL YOUNG DOLL WHO HAS ONLY EVER WANTED A HUMAN GIRL OF HER OWN TO LOVE, OR TO BE LOVED BY."
"AND THEN THERE'S THE *LEADER* OF THE MISFIT TOYS..."

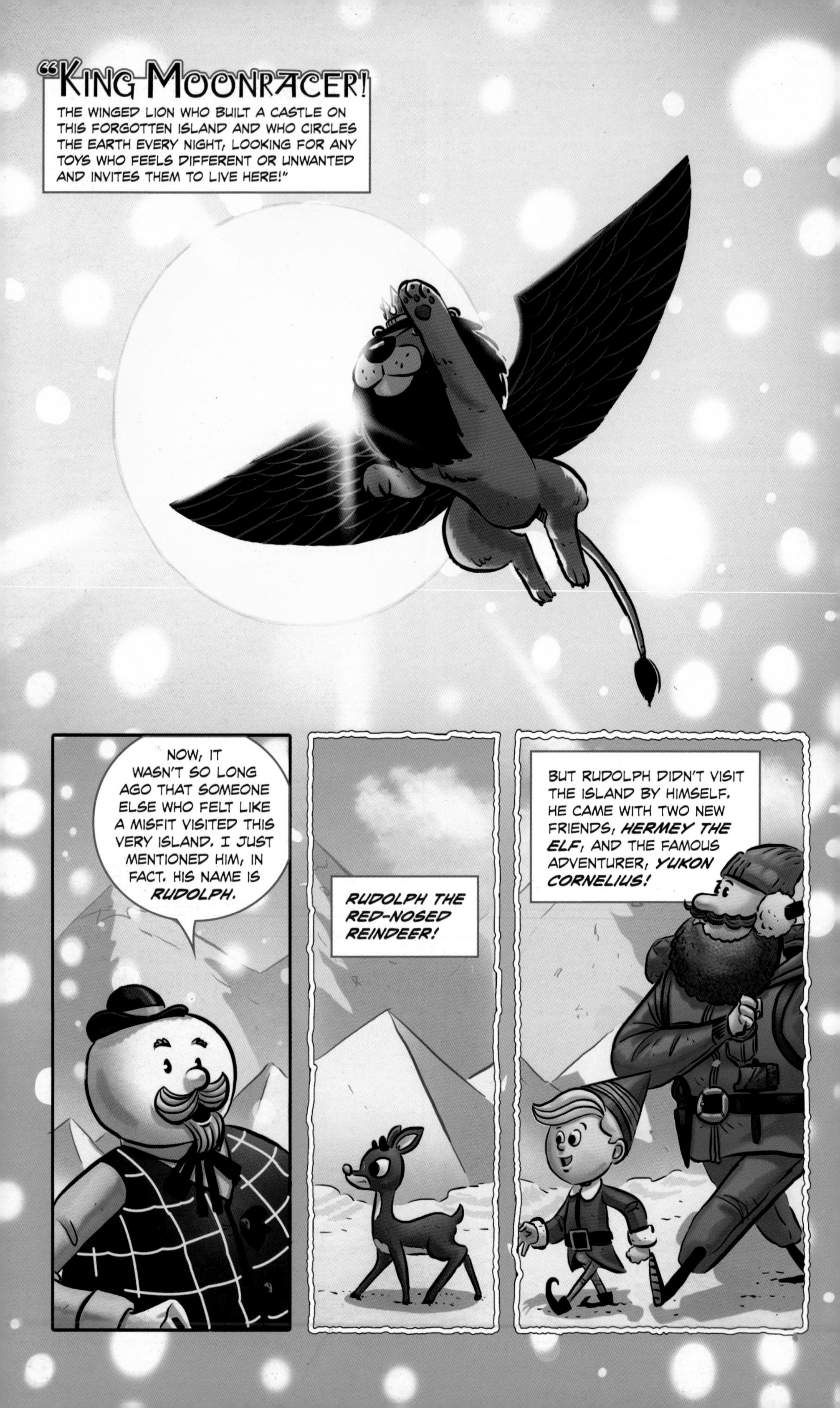
"KING MOONRACER!
THE WINGED LION WHO BUILT A CASTLE ON THIS FORGOTTEN ISLAND AND WHO CIRCLES THE EARTH EVERY NIGHT, LOOKING FOR ANY TOYS WHO FEELS DIFFERENT OR UNWANTED AND INVITES THEM TO LIVE HERE!"
NOW, IT WASN'T SO LONG AGO THAT SOMEONE ELSE WHO FELT LIKE A MISFIT VISITED THIS VERY ISLAND. I JUST MENTIONED HIM, IN FACT. HIS NAME IS RUDOLPH.
RUDOLPH THE RED-NOSED REINDEER!
BUT RUDOLPH DIDN'T VISIT THE ISLAND BY HIMSELF. HE CAME WITH TWO NEW FRIENDS, HERMEY THE ELF, AND THE FAMOUS ADVENTURER, YUKON CORNELIUS!

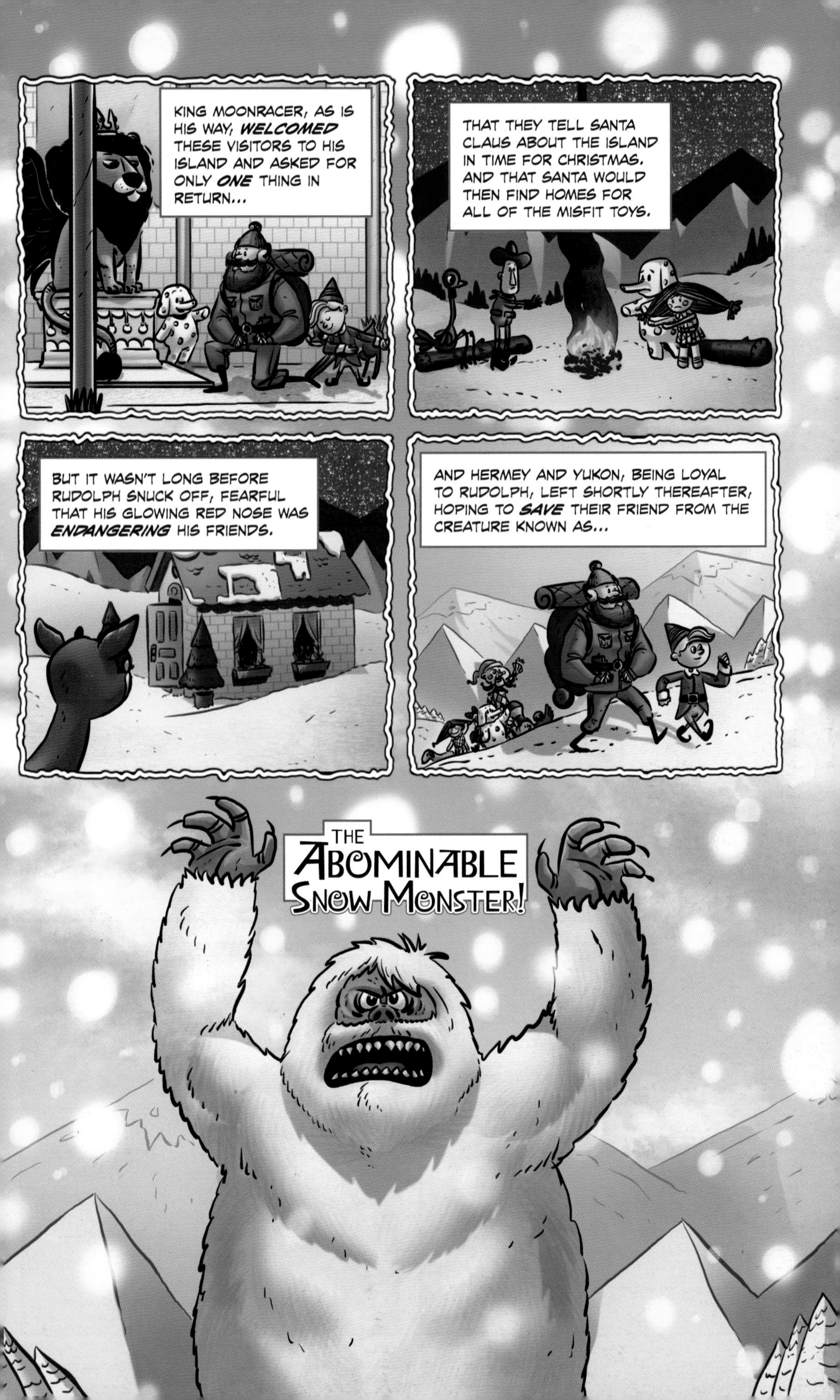
KING MOONRACER, AS IS HIS WAY, WELCOMED THESE VISITORS TO HIS ISLAND AND ASKED FOR ONLY ONE THING IN RETURN...
THAT THEY TELL SANTA CLAUS ABOUT THE ISLAND IN TIME FOR CHRISTMAS. AND THAT SANTA WOULD THEN FIND HOMES FOR ALL OF THE MISFIT TOYS.
BUT IT WASN'T LONG BEFORE RUDOLPH SNUCK OFF, FEARFUL THAT HIS GLOWING RED NOSE WAS ENDANGERING HIS FRIENDS.
AND HERMEY AND YUKON, BEING LOYAL TO RUDOLPH, LEFT SHORTLY THEREAFTER, HOPING TO SAVE THEIR FRIEND FROM THE CREATURE KNOWN AS...
THE ABOMINABLE SNOW MONSTER!

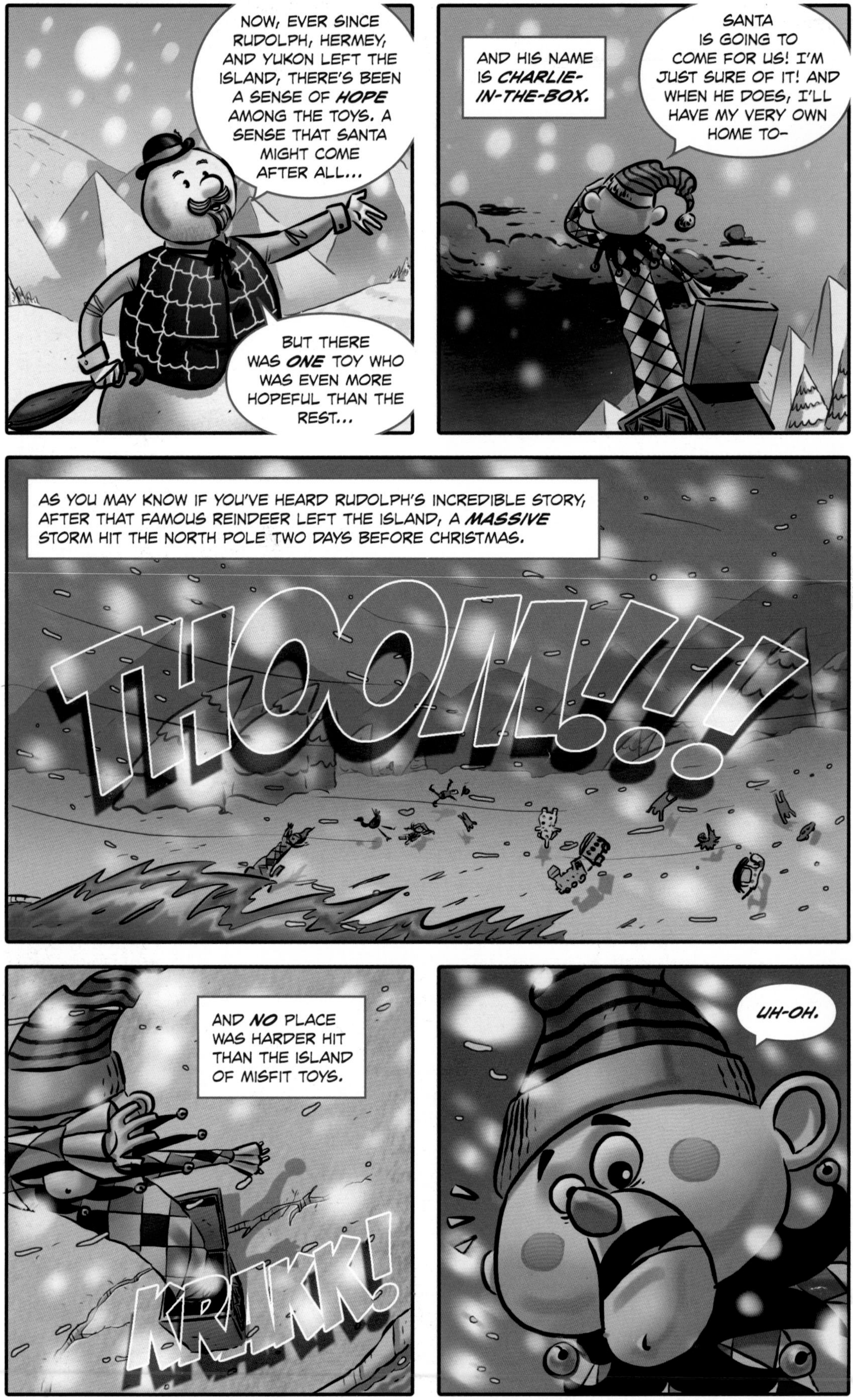
NOW, EVER SINCE RUDOLPH, HERMEY, AND YUKON LEFT THE ISLAND, THERE'S BEEN A SENSE OF HOPE AMONG THE TOYS. A SENSE THAT SANTA MIGHT COME AFTER ALL...
BUT THERE WAS ONE TOY WHO WAS EVEN MORE HOPEFUL THAN THE REST...
AND HIS NAME IS CHARLIE-IN-THE-BOX.
SANTA IS GOING TO COME FOR US! I'M JUST SURE OF IT! AND WHEN HE DOES, I'LL HAVE MY VERY OWN HOME TO-
AS YOU MAY KNOW IF YOU'VE HEARD RUDOLPH'S INCREDIBLE STORY, AFTER THAT FAMOUS REINDEER LEFT THE ISLAND, A MASSIVE STORM HIT THE NORTH POLE TWO DAYS BEFORE CHRISTMAS.
THOOM!!!
AND NO PLACE WAS HARDER HIT THAN THE ISLAND OF MISFIT TOYS.
KRAKK!
UH-OH.

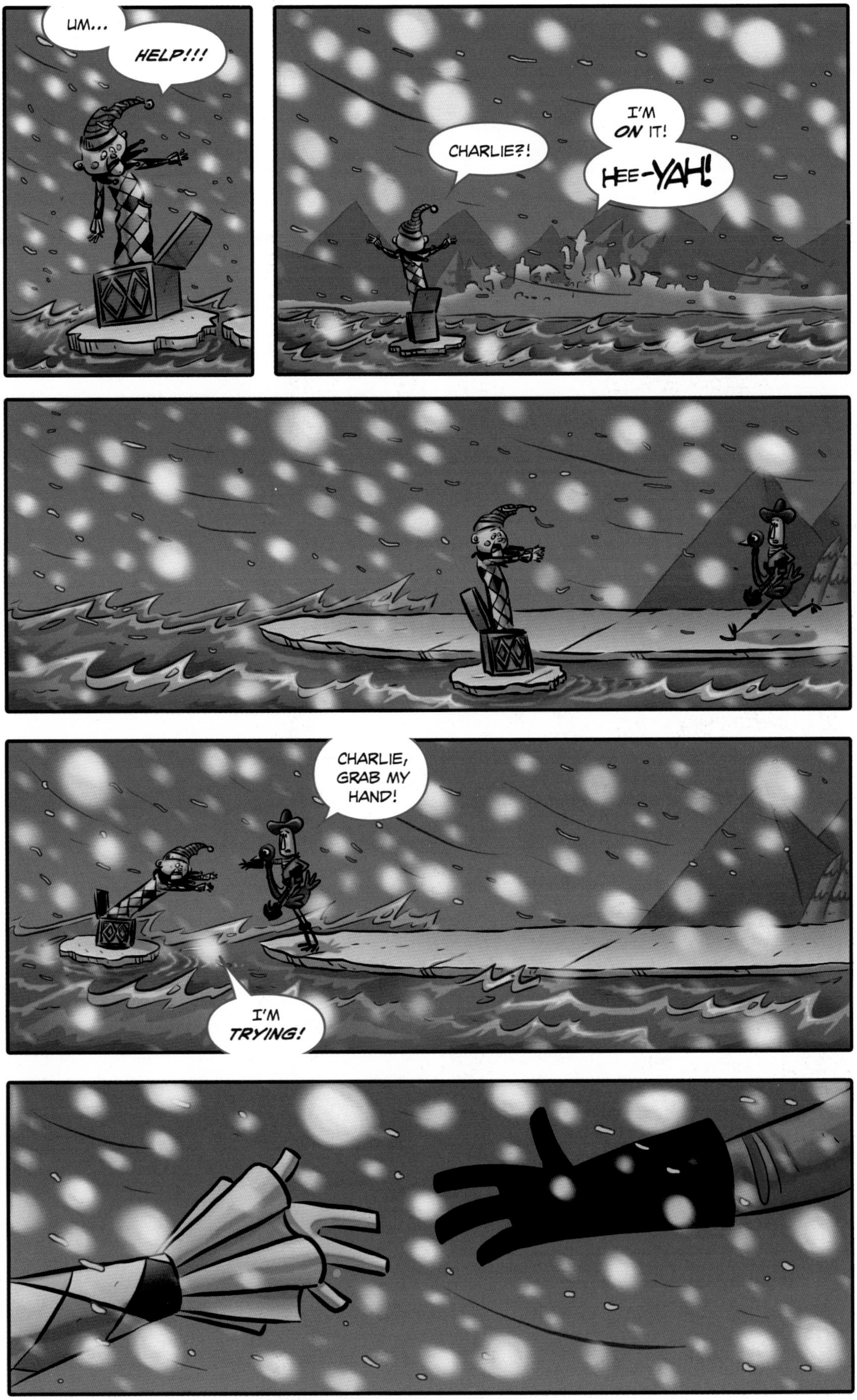

UM...
HELP!!!
CHARLIE?!
I'M ON IT!
HEE-YAH!
CHARLIE, GRAB MY HAND!
I'M TRYING!

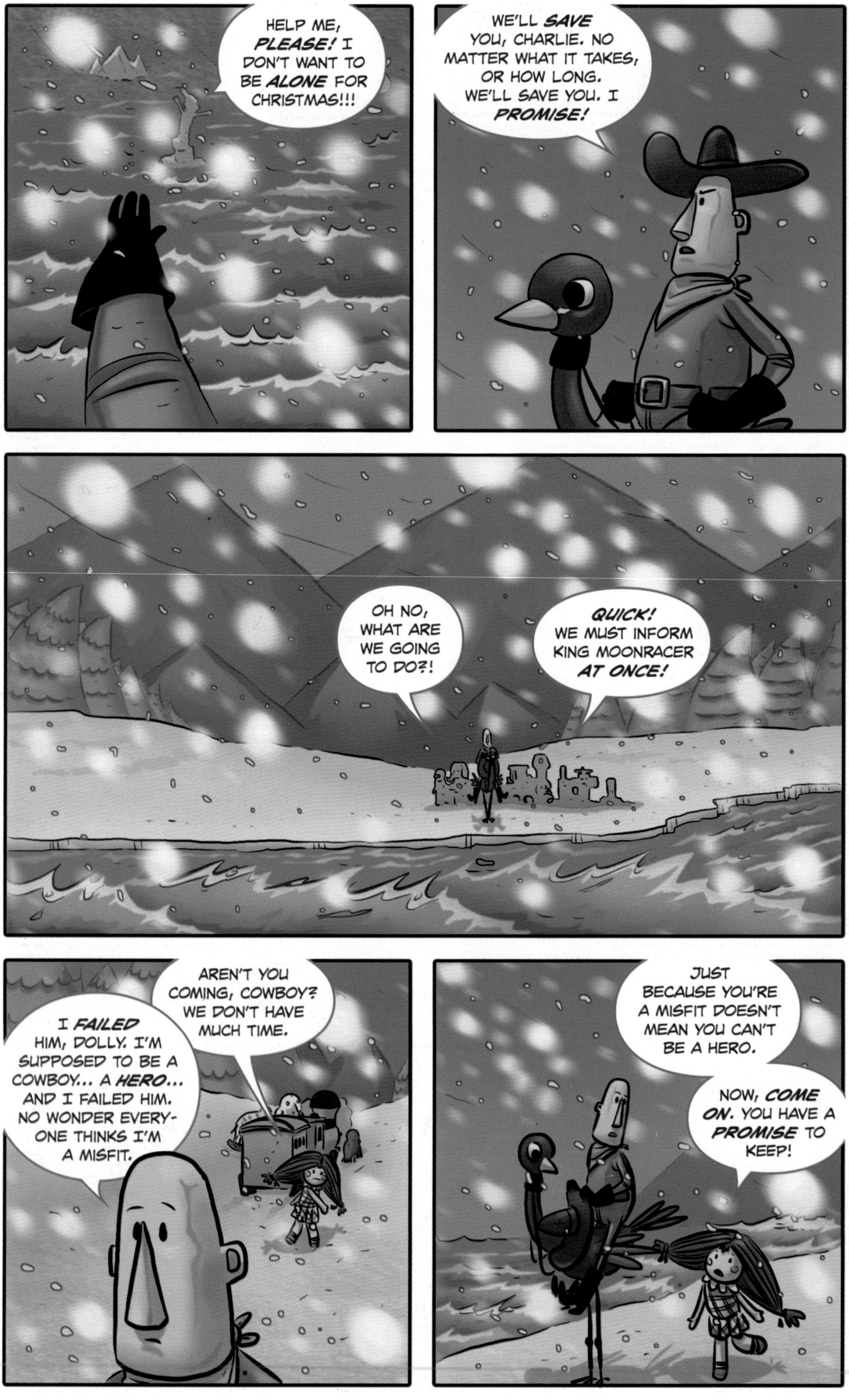
HELP ME, PLEASE! I DON'T WANT TO BE ALONE FOR CHRISTMAS!!!
WE'LL SAVE YOU, CHARLIE. NO MATTER WHAT IT TAKES, OR HOW LONG. WE'LL SAVE YOU. I PROMISE!
OH NO, WHAT ARE WE GOING TO DO?!
QUICK! WE MUST INFORM KING MOONRACER AT ONCE!
AREN'T YOU COMING, COWBOY? WE DON'T HAVE MUCH TIME.
I FAILED HIM, DOLLY. I'M SUPPOSED TO BE A COWBOY... A HERO... AND I FAILED HIM. NO WONDER EVERY-ONE THINKS I'M A MISFIT.
JUST BECAUSE YOU'RE A MISFIT DOESN'T MEAN YOU CAN'T BE A HERO.
NOW, COME ON. YOU HAVE A PROMISE TO KEEP!

"KING MOONRACER! KING MOONRACER!!"

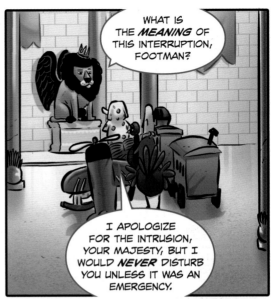

WHAT IS THE *MEANING* OF THIS INTERRUPTION, FOOTMAN?

I APOLOGIZE FOR THE INTRUSION, YOUR MAJESTY, BUT I WOULD *NEVER* DISTURB YOU UNLESS IT WAS AN EMERGENCY.

IT'S JUST THAT... CHARLIE-IN-THE-BOX IS *GONE!* HE WAS SWEPT OUT TO SEA WHEN THE STORM HIT!

WHAT?! THIS IS SERIOUS INDEED!

WHAT SHOULD WE *DO,* YOUR MAJESTY?

THIS STORM IS THE *WORST* TO EVER HIT THE ISLAND.

EVEN IF I *COULD* FLY, I WOULDN'T WANT TO RISK IT!

AND CHRISTMAS IS ALMOST HERE!

SILENCE!

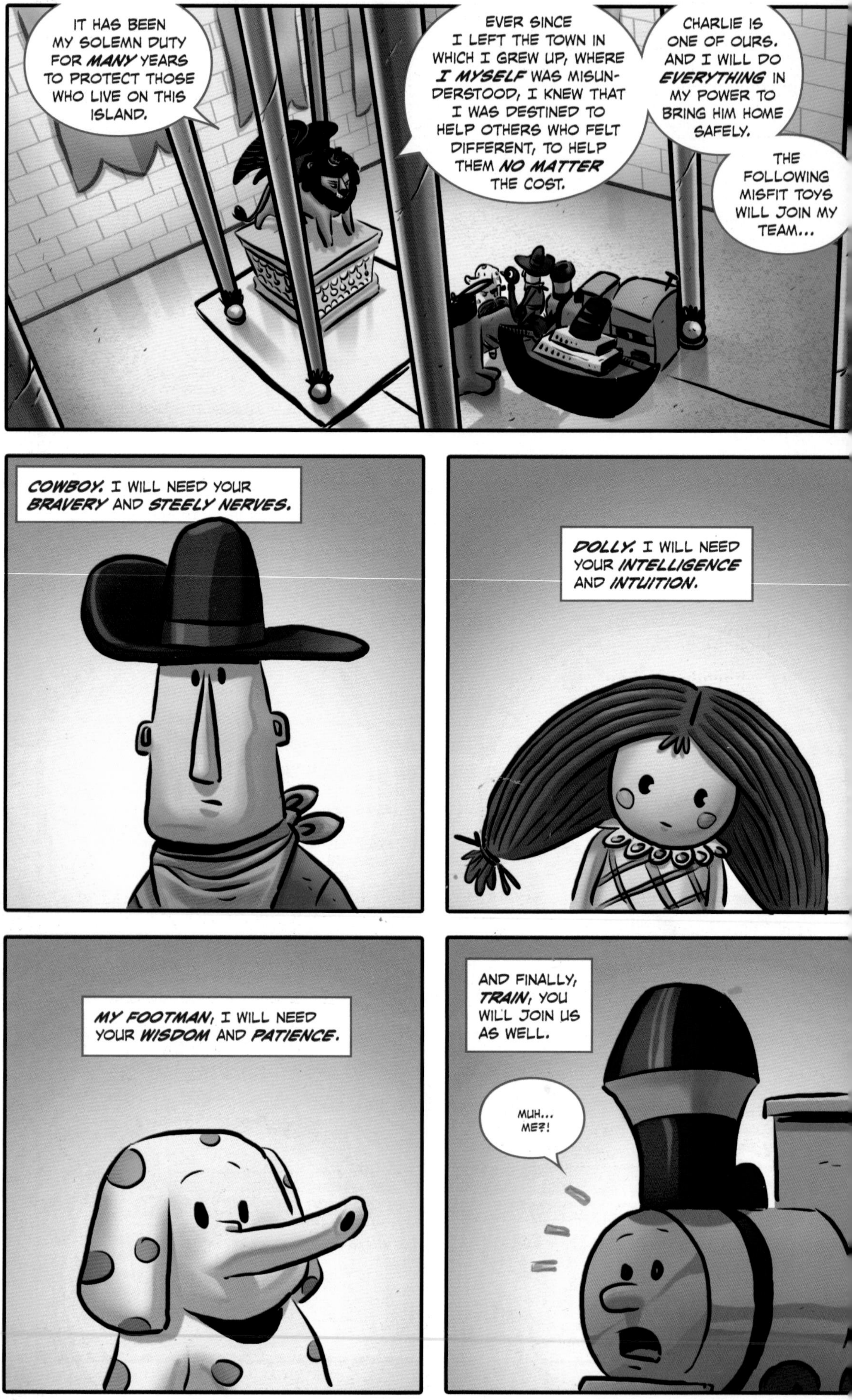

IT HAS BEEN MY SOLEMN DUTY FOR MANY YEARS TO PROTECT THOSE WHO LIVE ON THIS ISLAND.
EVER SINCE I LEFT THE TOWN IN WHICH I GREW UP, WHERE I MYSELF WAS MISUNDERSTOOD, I KNEW THAT I WAS DESTINED TO HELP OTHERS WHO FELT DIFFERENT, TO HELP THEM NO MATTER THE COST.
CHARLIE IS ONE OF OURS. AND I WILL DO EVERYTHING IN MY POWER TO BRING HIM HOME SAFELY.
THE FOLLOWING MISFIT TOYS WILL JOIN MY TEAM...
COWBOY. I WILL NEED YOUR BRAVERY AND STEELY NERVES.
DOLLY. I WILL NEED YOUR INTELLIGENCE AND INTUITION.
MY FOOTMAN, I WILL NEED YOUR WISDOM AND PATIENCE.
AND FINALLY, TRAIN, YOU WILL JOIN US AS WELL.
MUH... ME?!

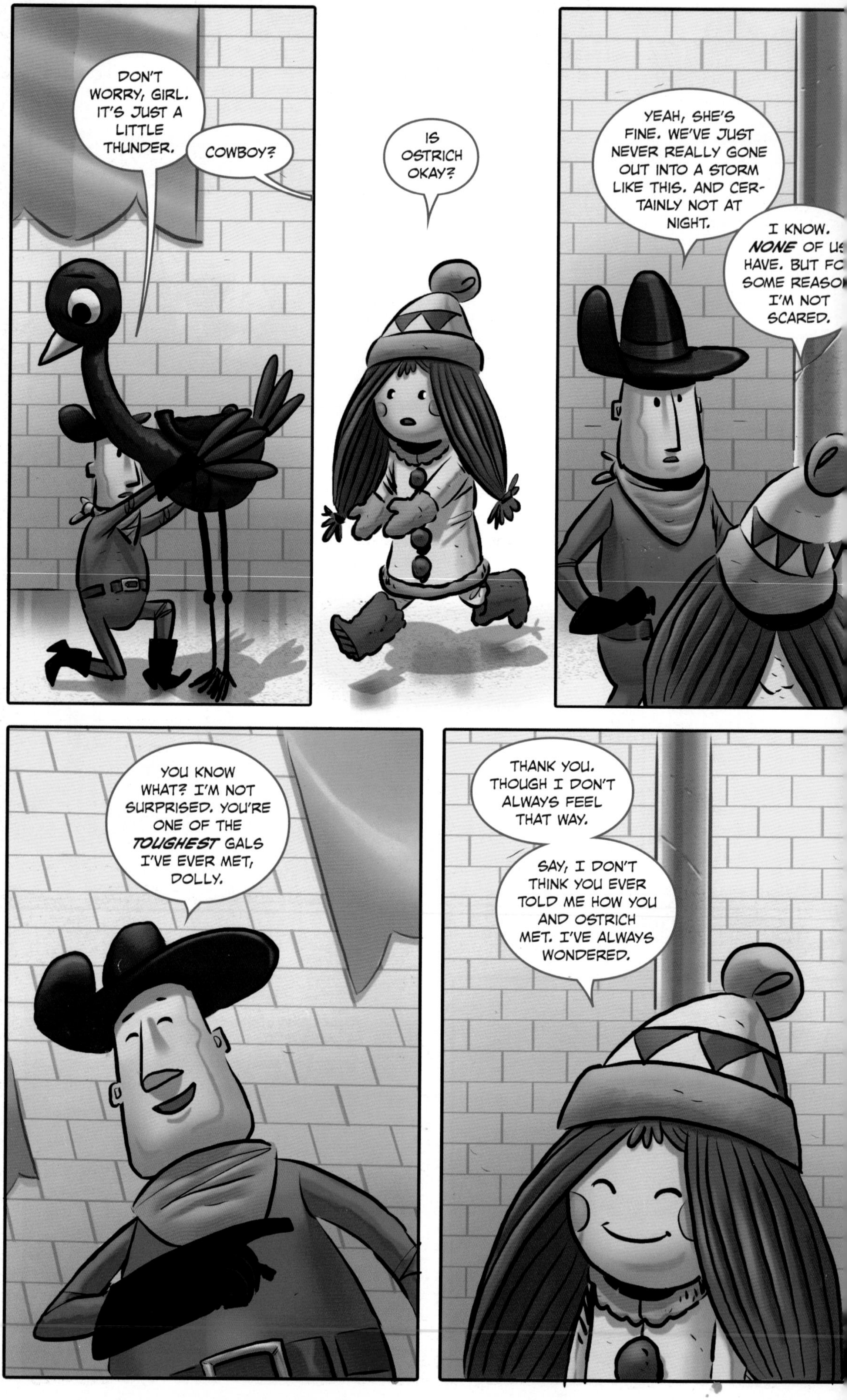
DON'T WORRY, GIRL. IT'S JUST A LITTLE THUNDER.
COWBOY?
IS OSTRICH OKAY?
YEAH, SHE'S FINE. WE'VE JUST NEVER REALLY GONE OUT INTO A STORM LIKE THIS. AND CER-TAINLY NOT AT NIGHT.
I KNOW. NONE OF US HAVE. BUT FO SOME REASO I'M NOT SCARED.
YOU KNOW WHAT? I'M NOT SURPRISED. YOU'RE ONE OF THE TOUGHEST GALS I'VE EVER MET, DOLLY.
THANK YOU. THOUGH I DON'T ALWAYS FEEL THAT WAY.
SAY, I DON'T THINK YOU EVER TOLD ME HOW YOU AND OSTRICH MET. I'VE ALWAYS WONDERED.

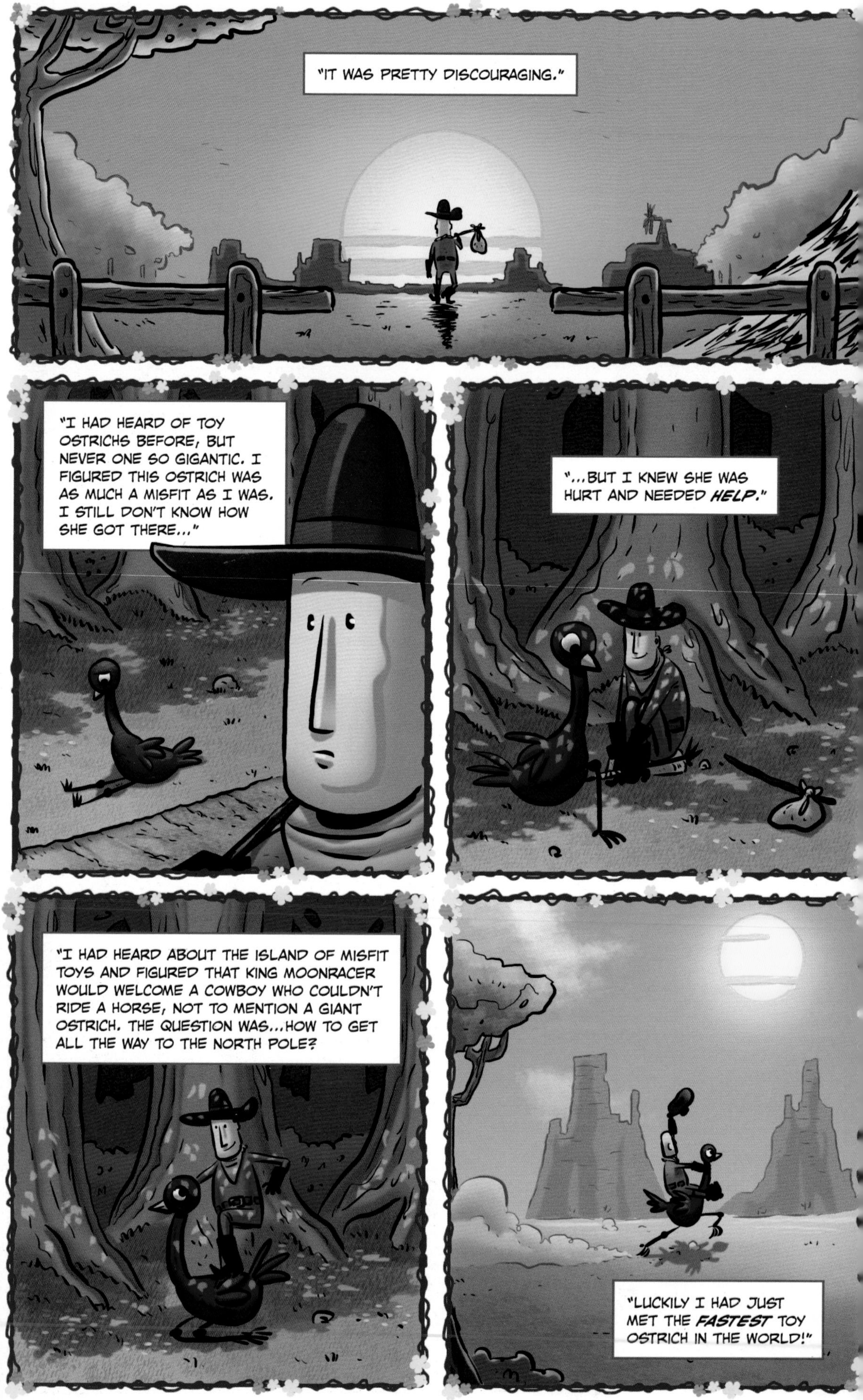
"IT WAS PRETTY DISCOURAGING."
"I HAD HEARD OF TOY OSTRICHS BEFORE, BUT NEVER ONE SO GIGANTIC. I FIGURED THIS OSTRICH WAS AS MUCH A MISFIT AS I WAS. I STILL DON'T KNOW HOW SHE GOT THERE..."
"...BUT I KNEW SHE WAS HURT AND NEEDED HELP."
"I HAD HEARD ABOUT THE ISLAND OF MISFIT TOYS AND FIGURED THAT KING MOONRACER WOULD WELCOME A COWBOY WHO COULDN'T RIDE A HORSE, NOT TO MENTION A GIANT OSTRICH. THE QUESTION WAS...HOW TO GET ALL THE WAY TO THE NORTH POLE?
"LUCKILY I HAD JUST MET THE FASTEST TOY OSTRICH IN THE WORLD!"

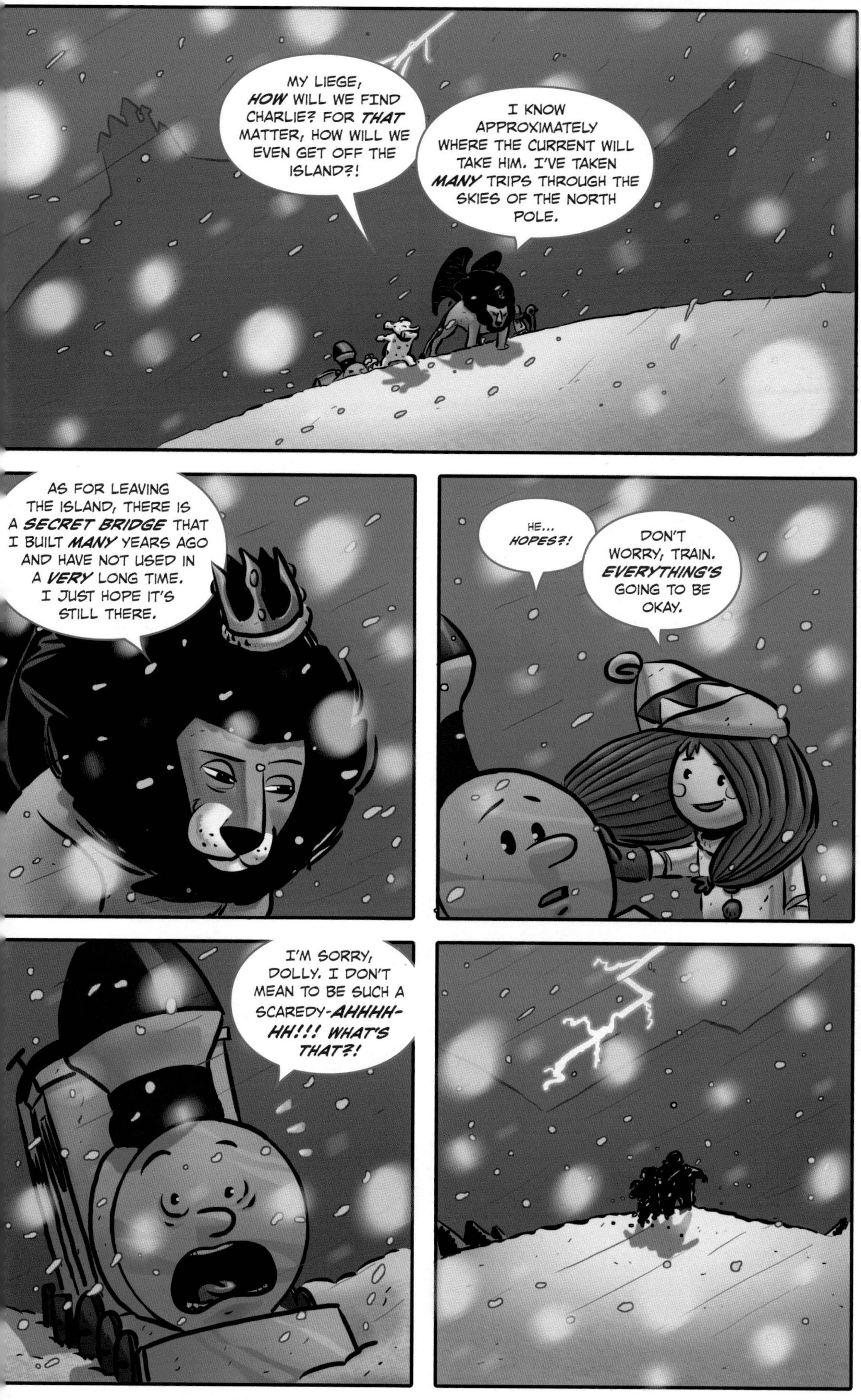
MY LIEGE, HOW WILL WE FIND CHARLIE? FOR THAT MATTER, HOW WILL WE EVEN GET OFF THE ISLAND?!
I KNOW APPROXIMATELY WHERE THE CURRENT WILL TAKE HIM. I'VE TAKEN MANY TRIPS THROUGH THE SKIES OF THE NORTH POLE.
AS FOR LEAVING THE ISLAND, THERE IS A SECRET BRIDGE THAT I BUILT MANY YEARS AGO AND HAVE NOT USED IN A VERY LONG TIME. I JUST HOPE IT'S STILL THERE.
HE... HOPES?!
DON'T WORRY, TRAIN. EVERYTHING'S GOING TO BE OKAY.
I'M SORRY, DOLLY. I DON'T MEAN TO BE SUCH A SCAREDY-AHHHH-HH!!! WHAT'S THAT?!

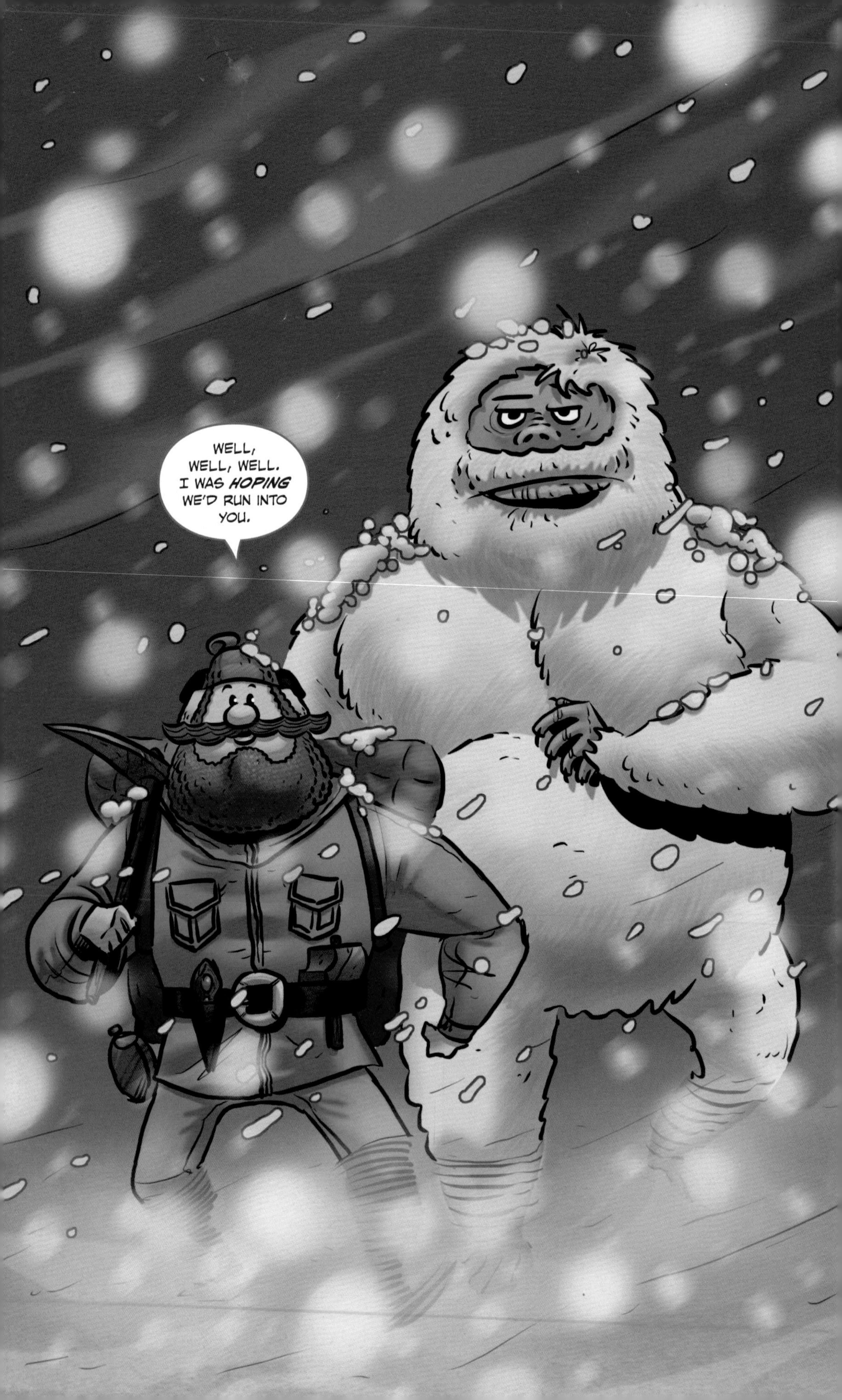
WELL, WELL, WELL. I WAS *HOPING* WE'D RUN INTO YOU.

CHAPTER TWO

SEPARATED!

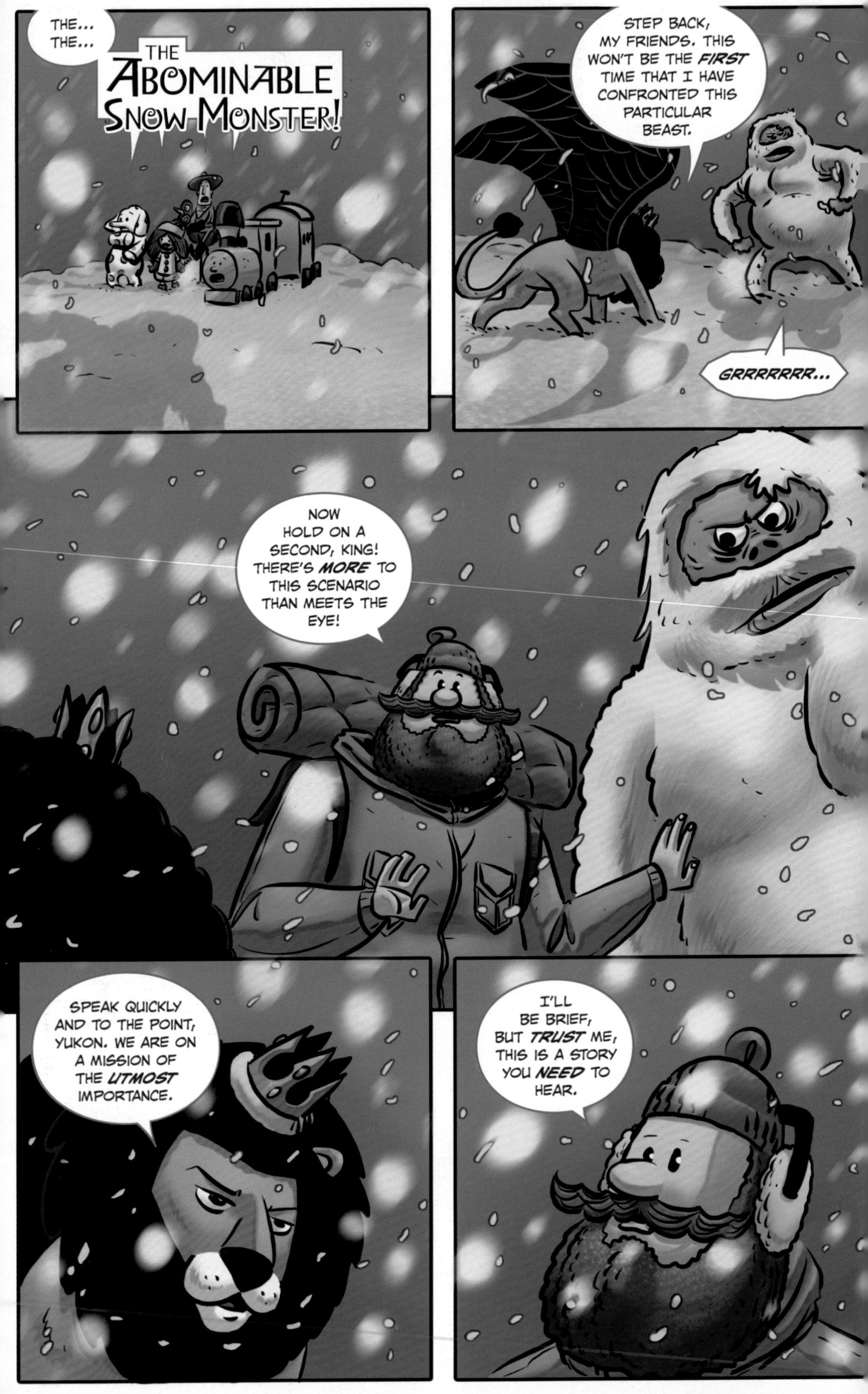
THE... THE...
THE ABOMINABLE SNOW MONSTER!
STEP BACK, MY FRIENDS. THIS WON'T BE THE FIRST TIME THAT I HAVE CONFRONTED THIS PARTICULAR BEAST.
GRRRRRRR...
NOW HOLD ON A SECOND, KING! THERE'S MORE TO THIS SCENARIO THAN MEETS THE EYE!
SPEAK QUICKLY AND TO THE POINT, YUKON. WE ARE ON A MISSION OF THE UTMOST IMPORTANCE.
I'LL BE BRIEF, BUT TRUST ME, THIS IS A STORY YOU NEED TO HEAR.

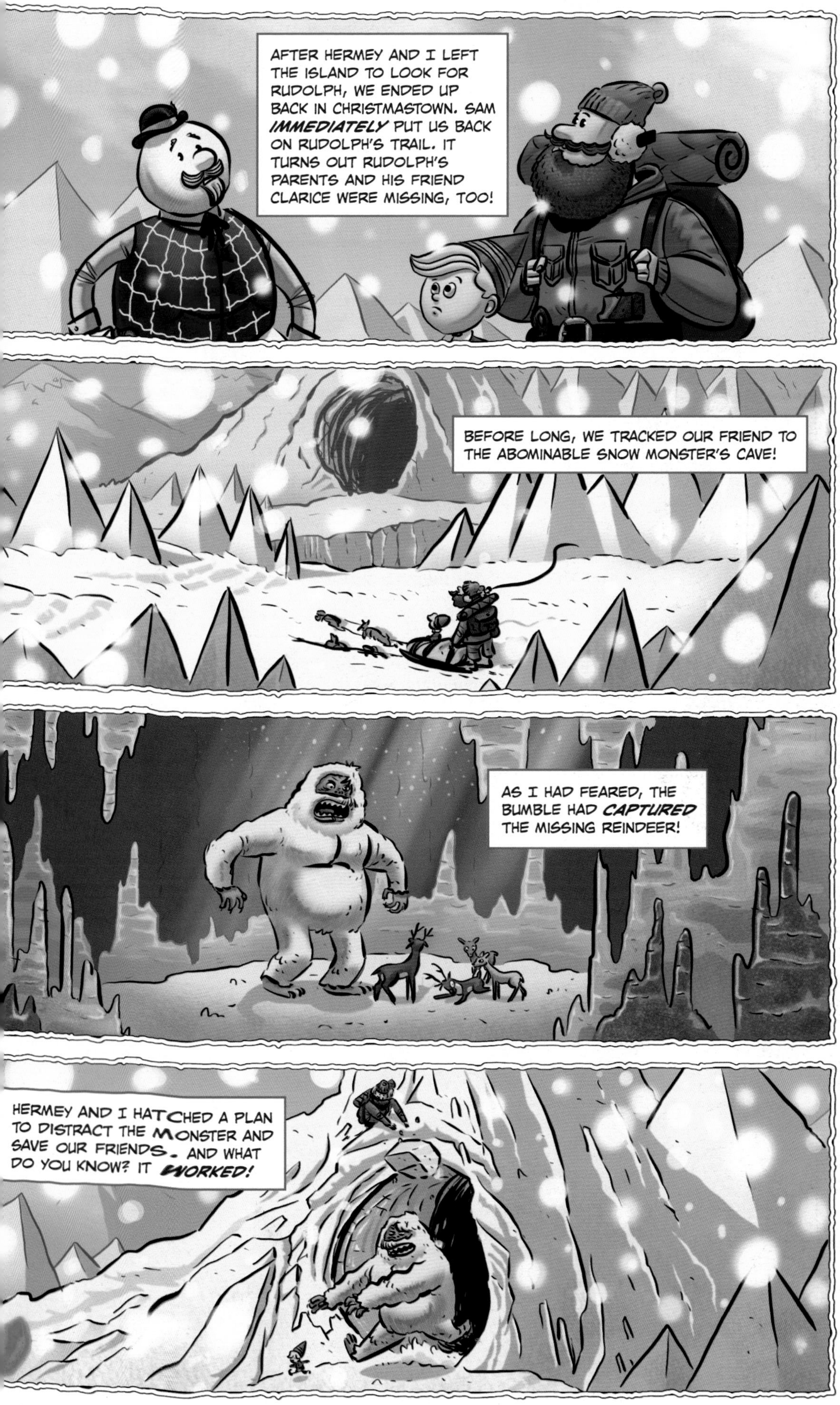
AFTER HERMEY AND I LEFT THE ISLAND TO LOOK FOR RUDOLPH, WE ENDED UP BACK IN CHRISTMASTOWN. SAM IMMEDIATELY PUT US BACK ON RUDOLPH'S TRAIL. IT TURNS OUT RUDOLPH'S PARENTS AND HIS FRIEND CLARICE WERE MISSING, TOO!
BEFORE LONG, WE TRACKED OUR FRIEND TO THE ABOMINABLE SNOW MONSTER'S CAVE!
AS I HAD FEARED, THE BUMBLE HAD CAPTURED THE MISSING REINDEER!
HERMEY AND I HATCHED A PLAN TO DISTRACT THE MONSTER AND SAVE OUR FRIENDS. AND WHAT DO YOU KNOW? IT WORKED!

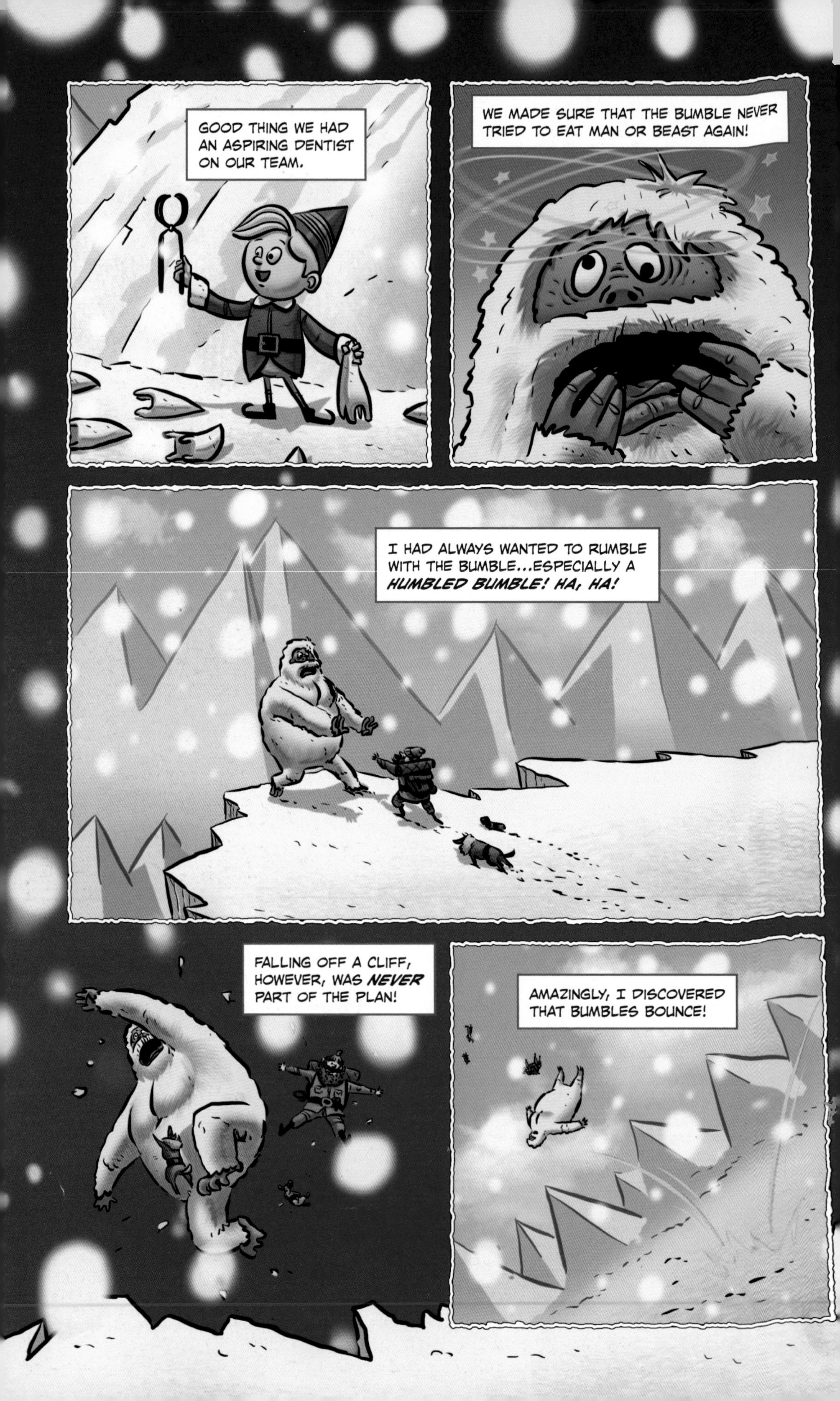
GOOD THING WE HAD AN ASPIRING DENTIST ON OUR TEAM.
WE MADE SURE THAT THE BUMBLE NEVER TRIED TO EAT MAN OR BEAST AGAIN!
I HAD ALWAYS WANTED TO RUMBLE WITH THE BUMBLE...ESPECIALLY A *HUMBLED BUMBLE! HA, HA!*
FALLING OFF A CLIFF, HOWEVER, WAS *NEVER* PART OF THE PLAN!
AMAZINGLY, I DISCOVERED THAT BUMBLES BOUNCE!

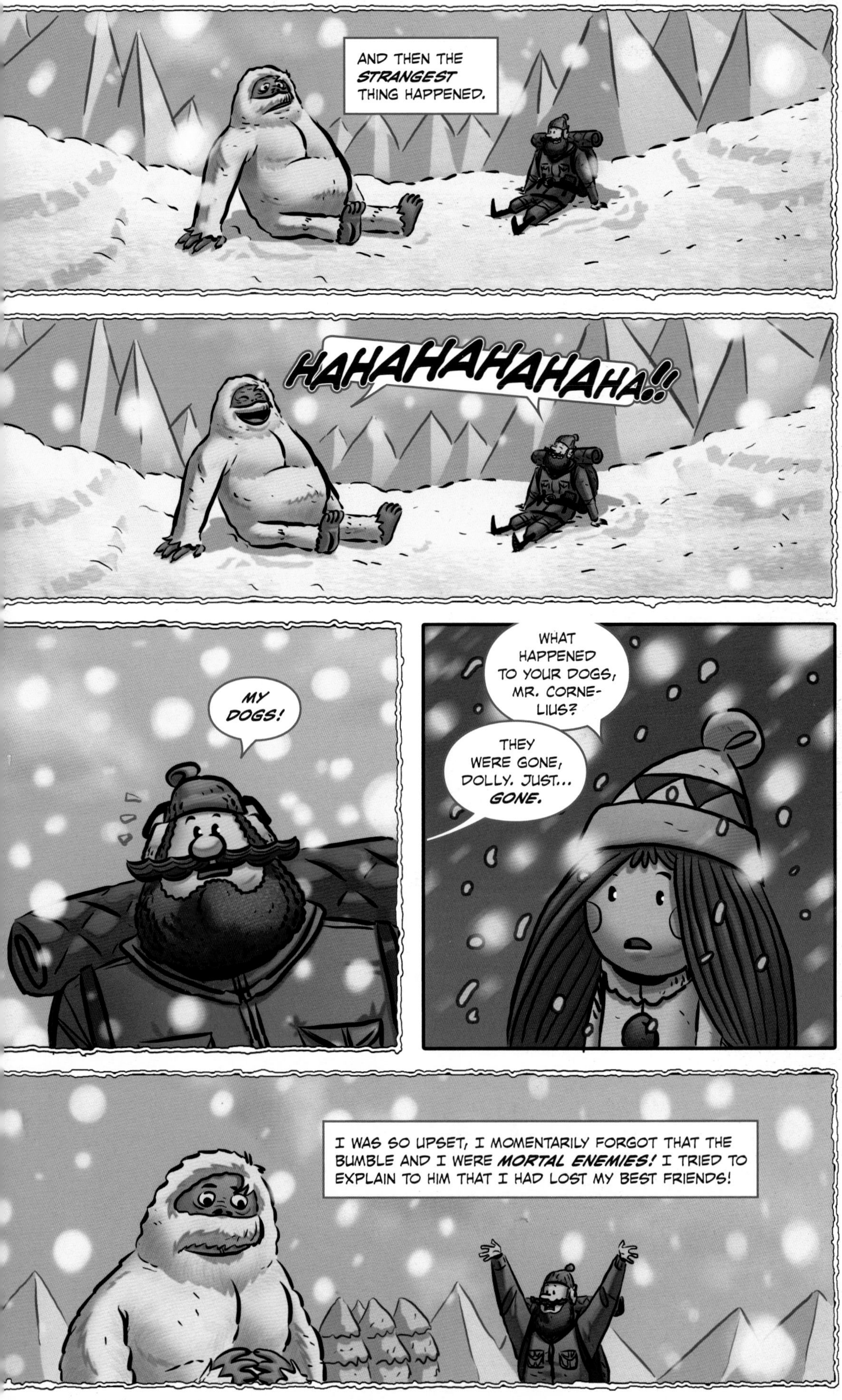
AND THEN THE STRANGEST THING HAPPENED.
HAHAHAHAHAHAHA!!
MY DOGS!
WHAT HAPPENED TO YOUR DOGS, MR. CORNELIUS?
THEY WERE GONE, DOLLY. JUST... GONE.
I WAS SO UPSET, I MOMENTARILY FORGOT THAT THE BUMBLE AND I WERE MORTAL ENEMIES! I TRIED TO EXPLAIN TO HIM THAT I HAD LOST MY BEST FRIENDS!

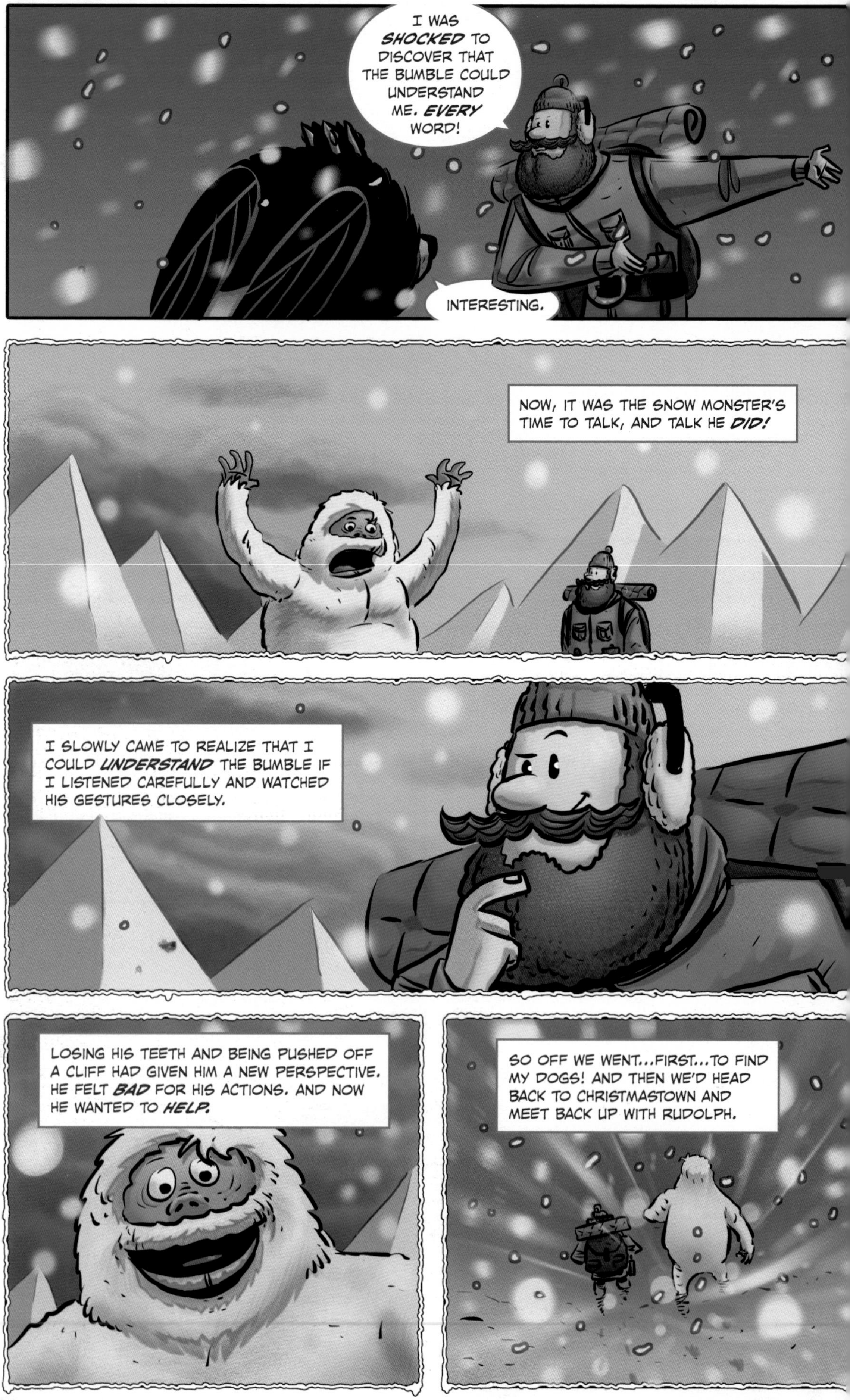
I WAS SHOCKED TO DISCOVER THAT THE BUMBLE COULD UNDERSTAND ME. EVERY WORD!
INTERESTING.
NOW, IT WAS THE SNOW MONSTER'S TIME TO TALK, AND TALK HE DID!
I SLOWLY CAME TO REALIZE THAT I COULD UNDERSTAND THE BUMBLE IF I LISTENED CAREFULLY AND WATCHED HIS GESTURES CLOSELY.
LOSING HIS TEETH AND BEING PUSHED OFF A CLIFF HAD GIVEN HIM A NEW PERSPECTIVE. HE FELT BAD FOR HIS ACTIONS. AND NOW HE WANTED TO HELP.
SO OFF WE WENT...FIRST...TO FIND MY DOGS! AND THEN WE'D HEAD BACK TO CHRISTMASTOWN AND MEET BACK UP WITH RUDOLPH.

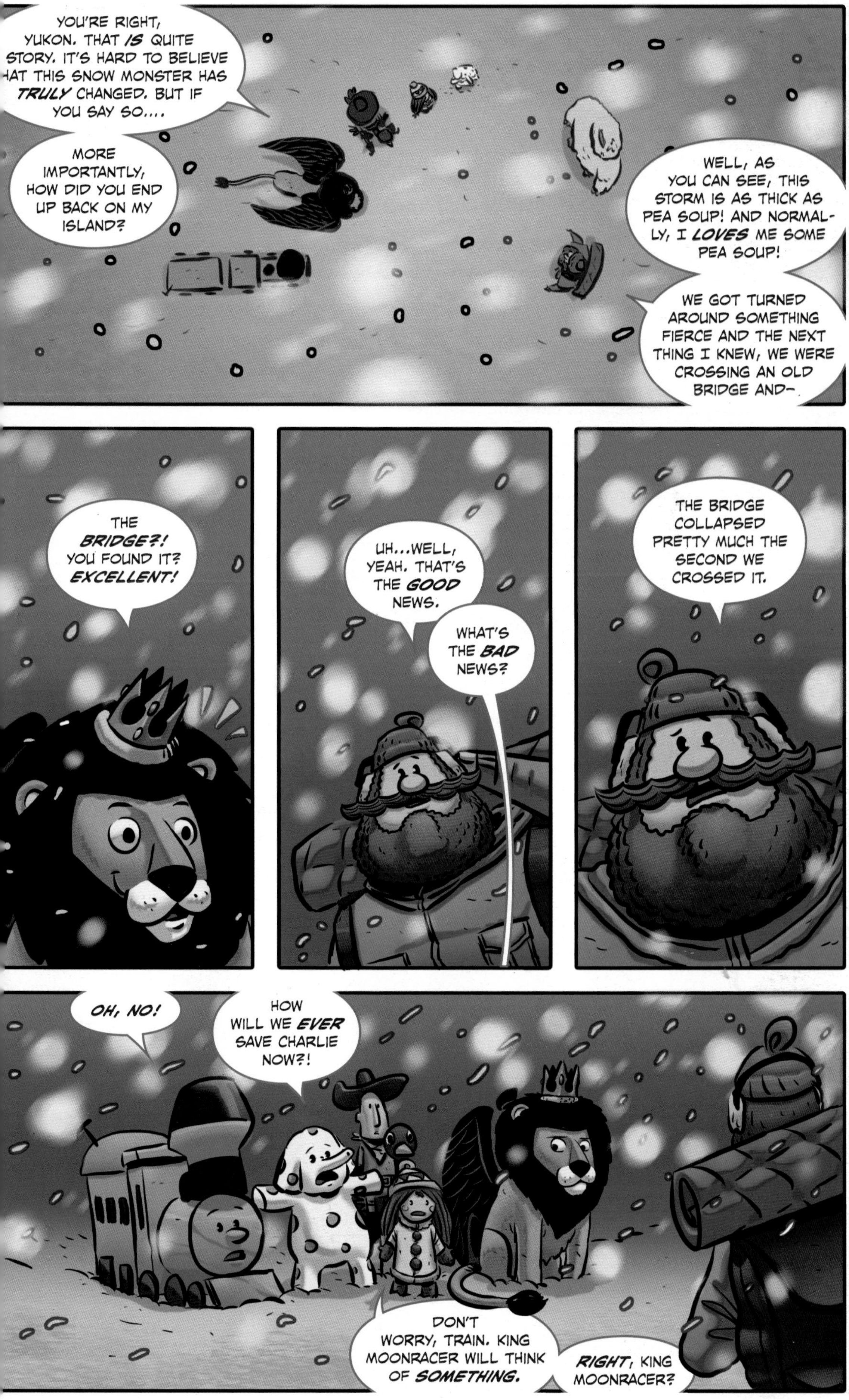
YOU'RE RIGHT, YUKON. THAT IS QUITE STORY. IT'S HARD TO BELIEVE HAT THIS SNOW MONSTER HAS TRULY CHANGED. BUT IF YOU SAY SO....
MORE IMPORTANTLY, HOW DID YOU END UP BACK ON MY ISLAND?
WELL, AS YOU CAN SEE, THIS STORM IS AS THICK AS PEA SOUP! AND NORMAL-LY, I LOVES ME SOME PEA SOUP!
WE GOT TURNED AROUND SOMETHING FIERCE AND THE NEXT THING I KNEW, WE WERE CROSSING AN OLD BRIDGE AND–
THE BRIDGE?! YOU FOUND IT? EXCELLENT!
UH...WELL, YEAH. THAT'S THE GOOD NEWS.
WHAT'S THE BAD NEWS?
THE BRIDGE COLLAPSED PRETTY MUCH THE SECOND WE CROSSED IT.
OH, NO!
HOW WILL WE EVER SAVE CHARLIE NOW?!
DON'T WORRY, TRAIN. KING MOONRACER WILL THINK OF SOMETHING.
RIGHT, KING MOONRACER?

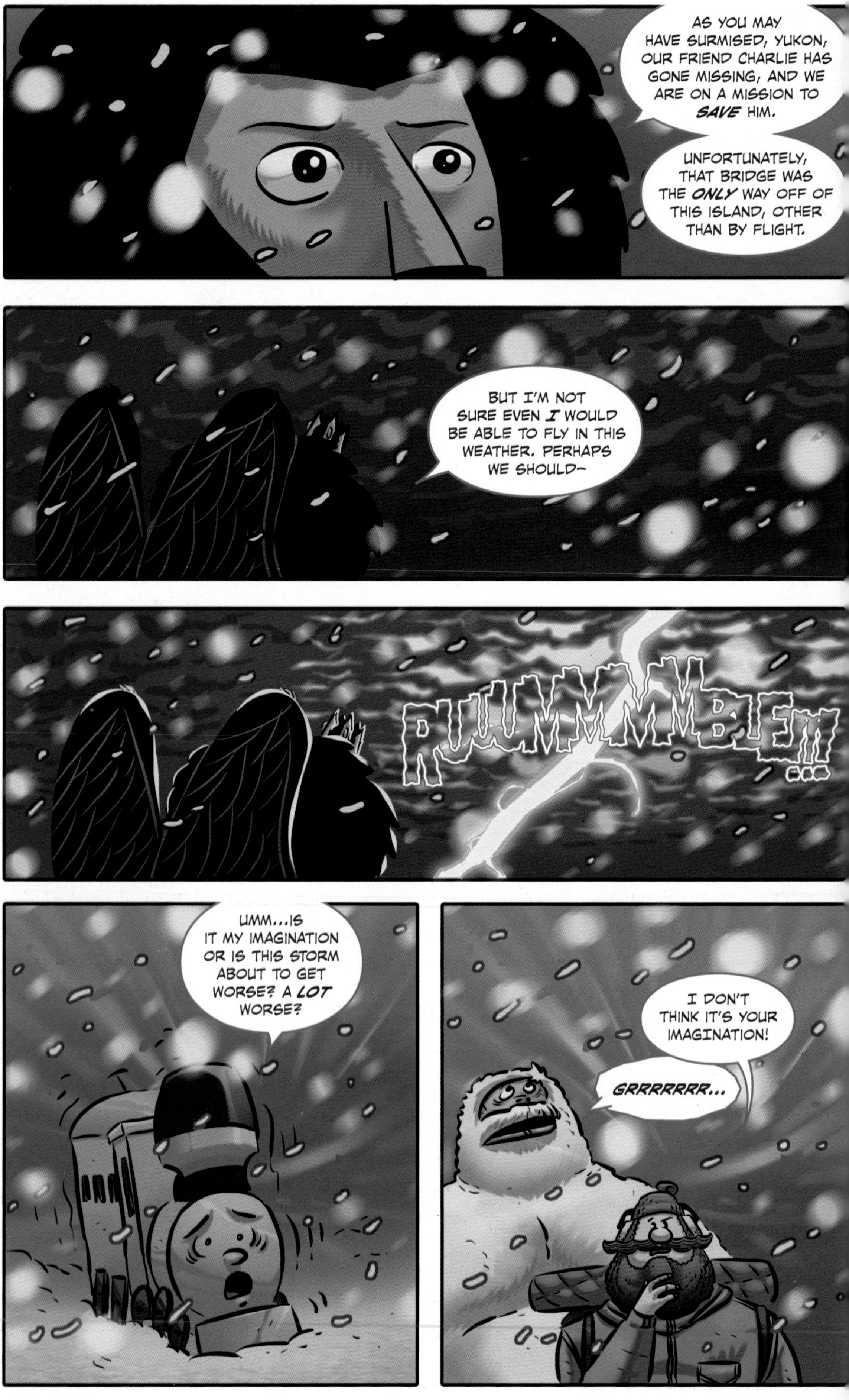
AS YOU MAY HAVE SURMISED, YUKON, OUR FRIEND CHARLIE HAS GONE MISSING, AND WE ARE ON A MISSION TO SAVE HIM.
UNFORTUNATELY, THAT BRIDGE WAS THE ONLY WAY OFF OF THIS ISLAND, OTHER THAN BY FLIGHT.
BUT I'M NOT SURE EVEN I WOULD BE ABLE TO FLY IN THIS WEATHER. PERHAPS WE SHOULD–
RUUUMMMMMBLE!!!
UMM...IS IT MY IMAGINATION OR IS THIS STORM ABOUT TO GET WORSE? A LOT WORSE?
I DON'T THINK IT'S YOUR IMAGINATION!
GRRRRRRR...

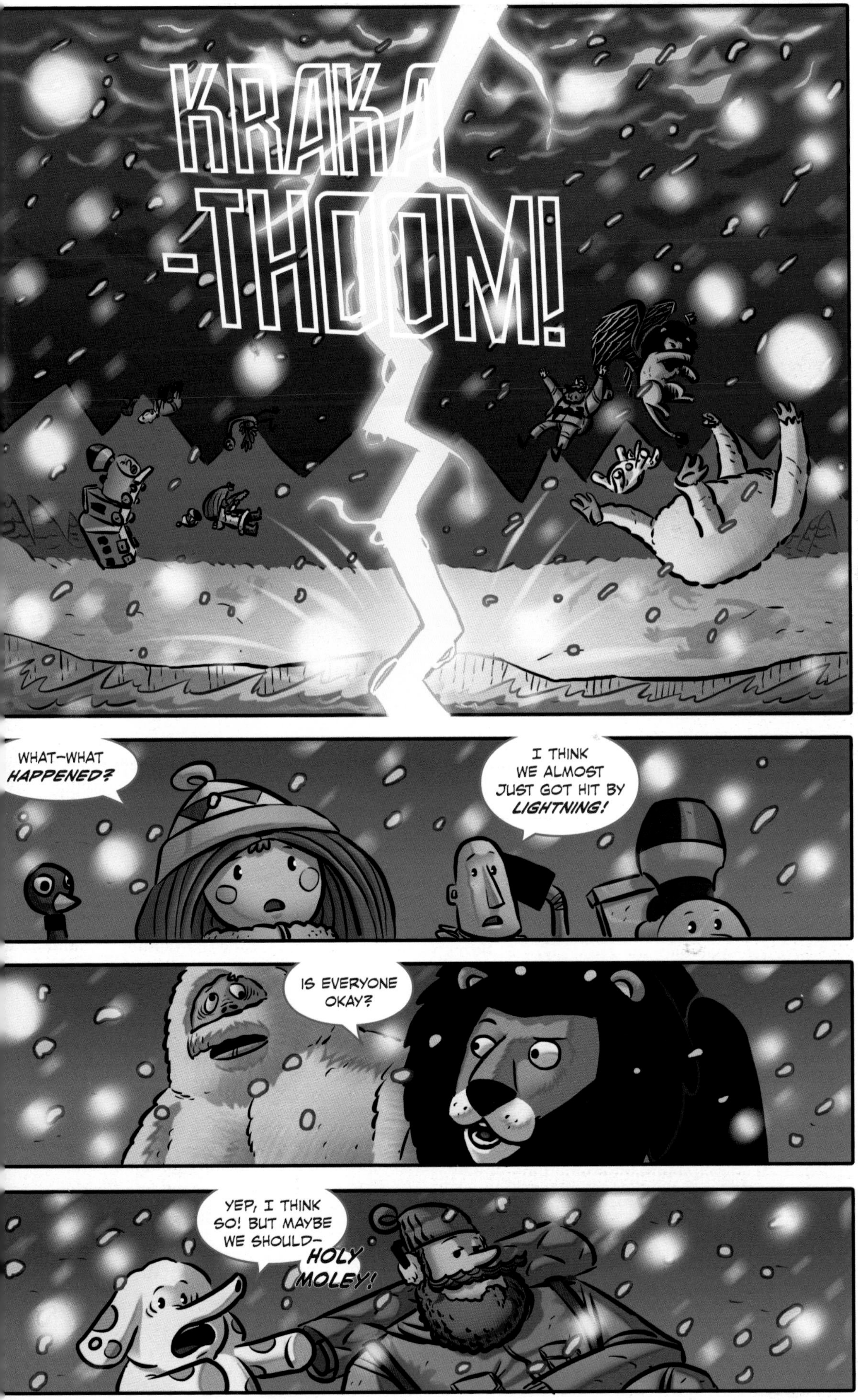
KRAKA-THOOM!
WHAT–WHAT HAPPENED?
I THINK WE ALMOST JUST GOT HIT BY LIGHTNING!
IS EVERYONE OKAY?
YEP, I THINK SO! BUT MAYBE WE SHOULD–
HOLY MOLEY!

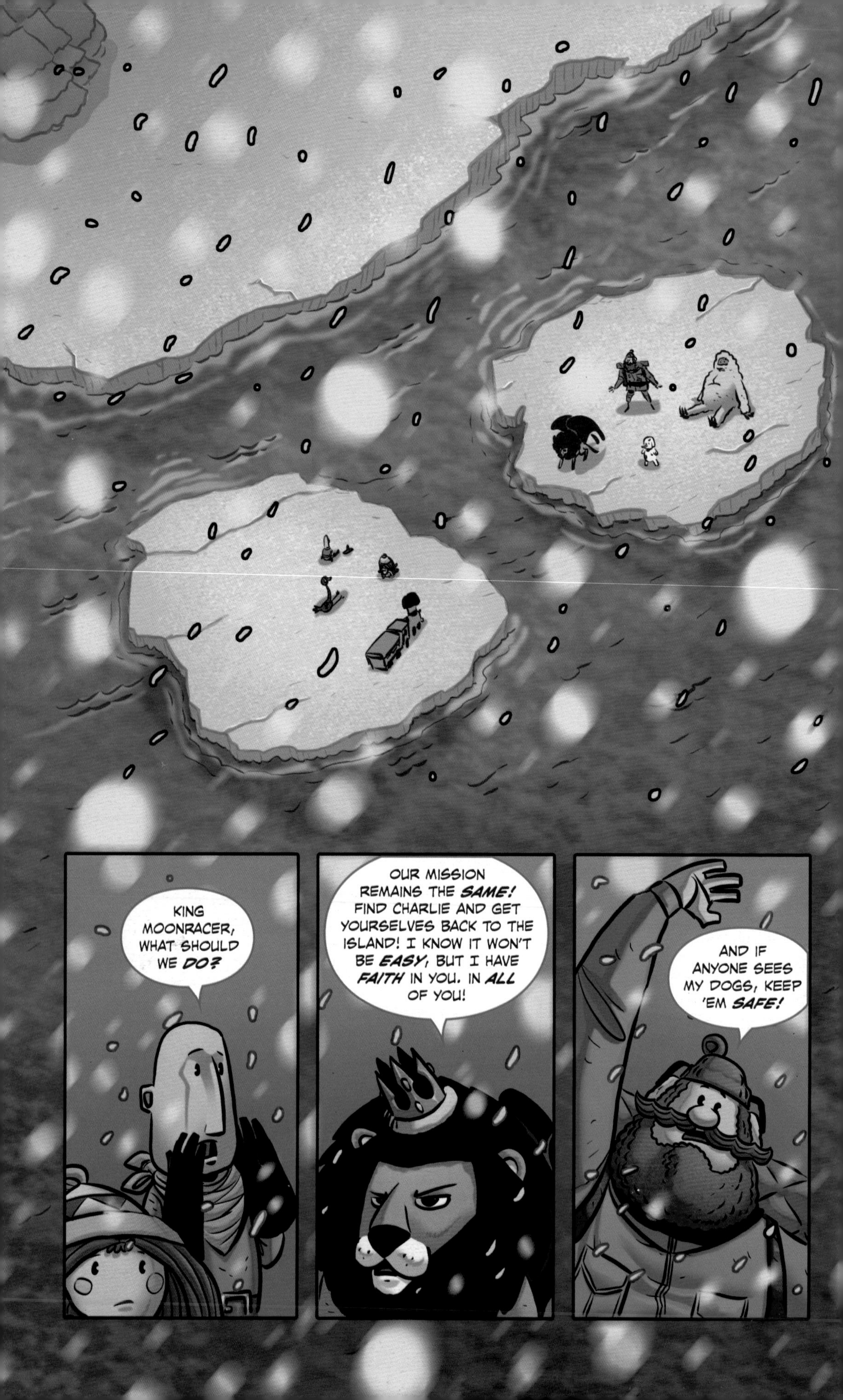
KING MOONRACER, WHAT SHOULD WE DO?
OUR MISSION REMAINS THE SAME! FIND CHARLIE AND GET YOURSELVES BACK TO THE ISLAND! I KNOW IT WON'T BE EASY, BUT I HAVE FAITH IN YOU. IN ALL OF YOU!
AND IF ANYONE SEES MY DOGS, KEEP 'EM SAFE!

CHAPTER THREE

DANGER AT EVERY TURN!

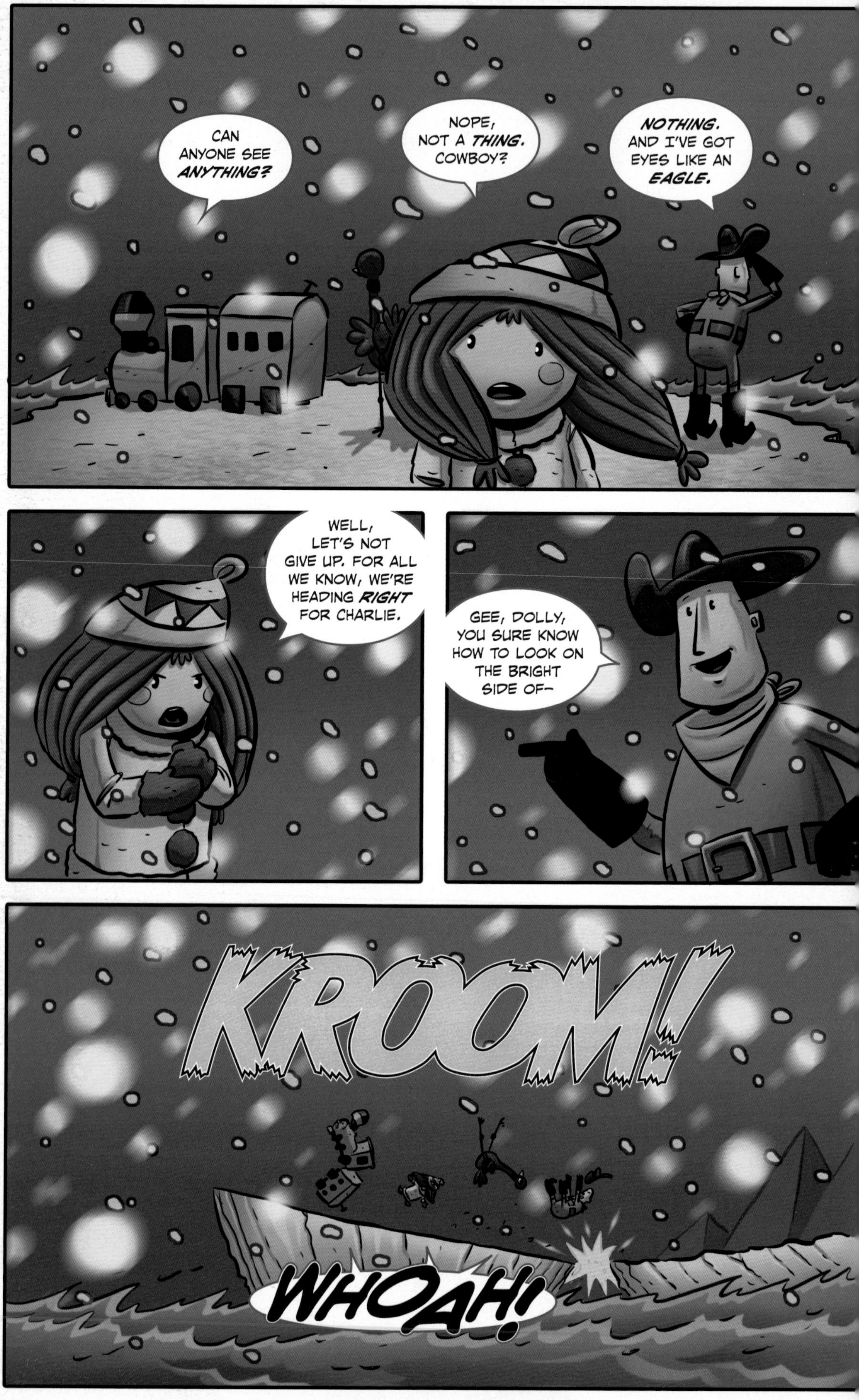
CAN ANYONE SEE *ANYTHING?*
NOPE, NOT A *THING.* COWBOY?
NOTHING. AND I'VE GOT EYES LIKE AN *EAGLE.*
WELL, LET'S NOT GIVE UP. FOR ALL WE KNOW, WE'RE HEADING *RIGHT* FOR CHARLIE.
GEE, DOLLY, YOU SURE KNOW HOW TO LOOK ON THE BRIGHT SIDE OF–
KROOM!
WHOAH!

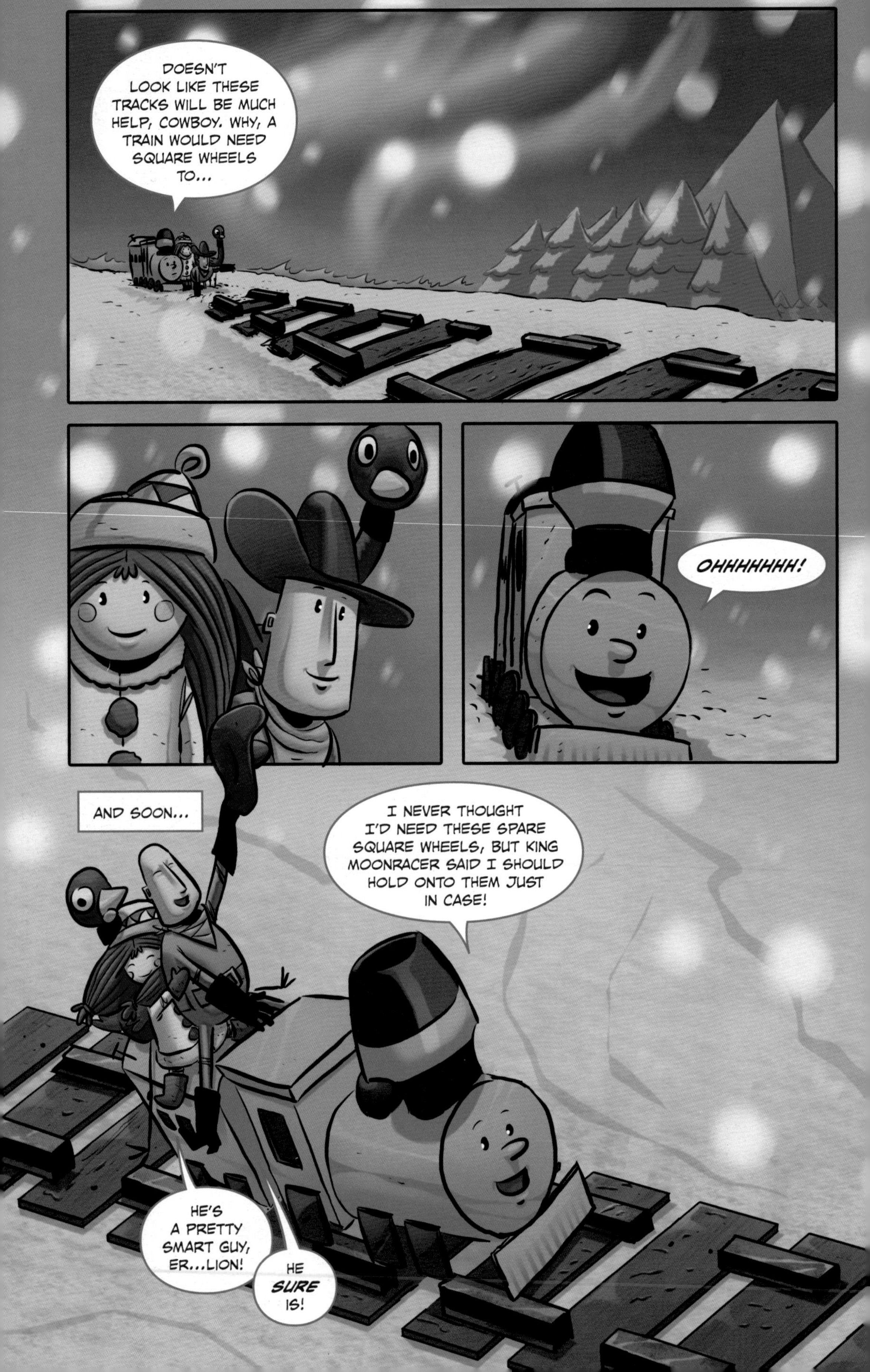
DOESN'T LOOK LIKE THESE TRACKS WILL BE MUCH HELP, COWBOY. WHY, A TRAIN WOULD NEED SQUARE WHEELS TO...
OHHHHHHH!
AND SOON...
I NEVER THOUGHT I'D NEED THESE SPARE SQUARE WHEELS, BUT KING MOONRACER SAID I SHOULD HOLD ONTO THEM JUST IN CASE!
HE'S A PRETTY SMART GUY, ER...LION!
HE *SURE* IS!

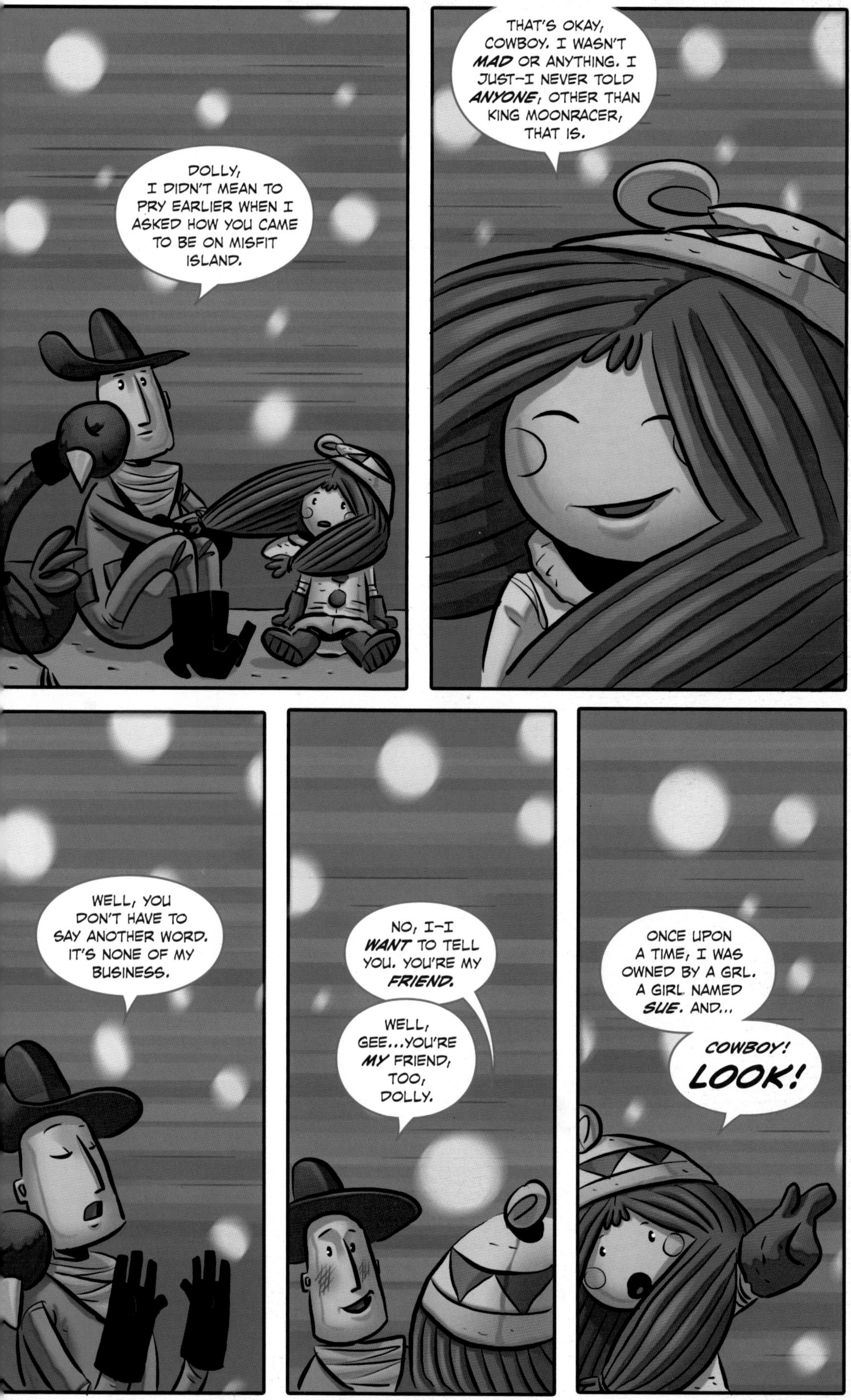
DOLLY, I DIDN'T MEAN TO PRY EARLIER WHEN I ASKED HOW YOU CAME TO BE ON MISFIT ISLAND.
THAT'S OKAY, COWBOY. I WASN'T MAD OR ANYTHING. I JUST--I NEVER TOLD ANYONE, OTHER THAN KING MOONRACER, THAT IS.
WELL, YOU DON'T HAVE TO SAY ANOTHER WORD. IT'S NONE OF MY BUSINESS.
NO, I--I WANT TO TELL YOU. YOU'RE MY FRIEND.
WELL, GEE...YOU'RE MY FRIEND, TOO, DOLLY.
ONCE UPON A TIME, I WAS OWNED BY A GRL. A GIRL NAMED SUE. AND...
COWBOY! LOOK!

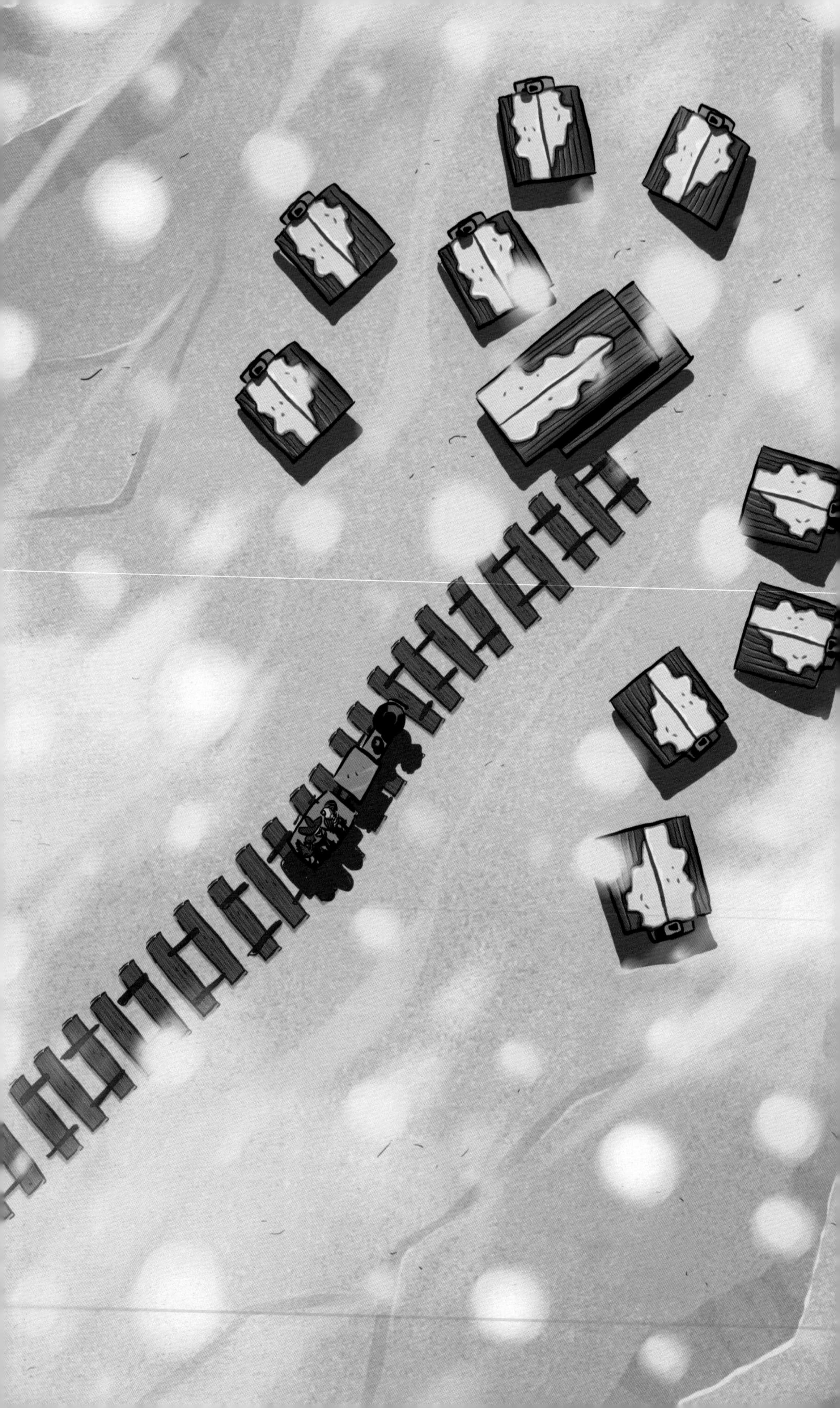

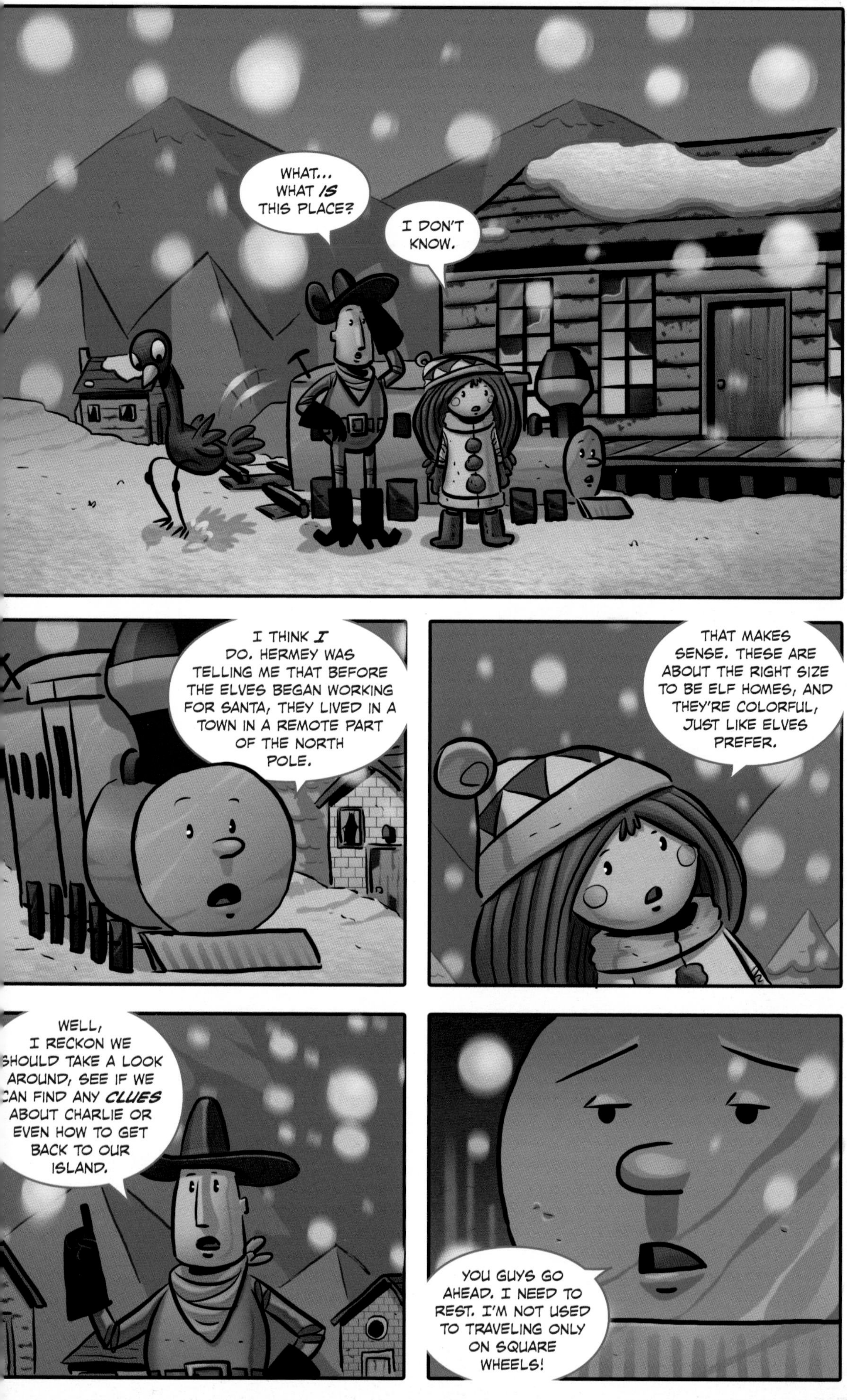
WHAT... WHAT *IS* THIS PLACE?
I DON'T KNOW.
I THINK *I* DO. HERMEY WAS TELLING ME THAT BEFORE THE ELVES BEGAN WORKING FOR SANTA, THEY LIVED IN A TOWN IN A REMOTE PART OF THE NORTH POLE.
THAT MAKES SENSE. THESE ARE ABOUT THE RIGHT SIZE TO BE ELF HOMES, AND THEY'RE COLORFUL, JUST LIKE ELVES PREFER.
WELL, I RECKON WE SHOULD TAKE A LOOK AROUND, SEE IF WE CAN FIND ANY *CLUES* ABOUT CHARLIE OR EVEN HOW TO GET BACK TO OUR ISLAND.
YOU GUYS GO AHEAD. I NEED TO REST. I'M NOT USED TO TRAVELING ONLY ON SQUARE WHEELS!

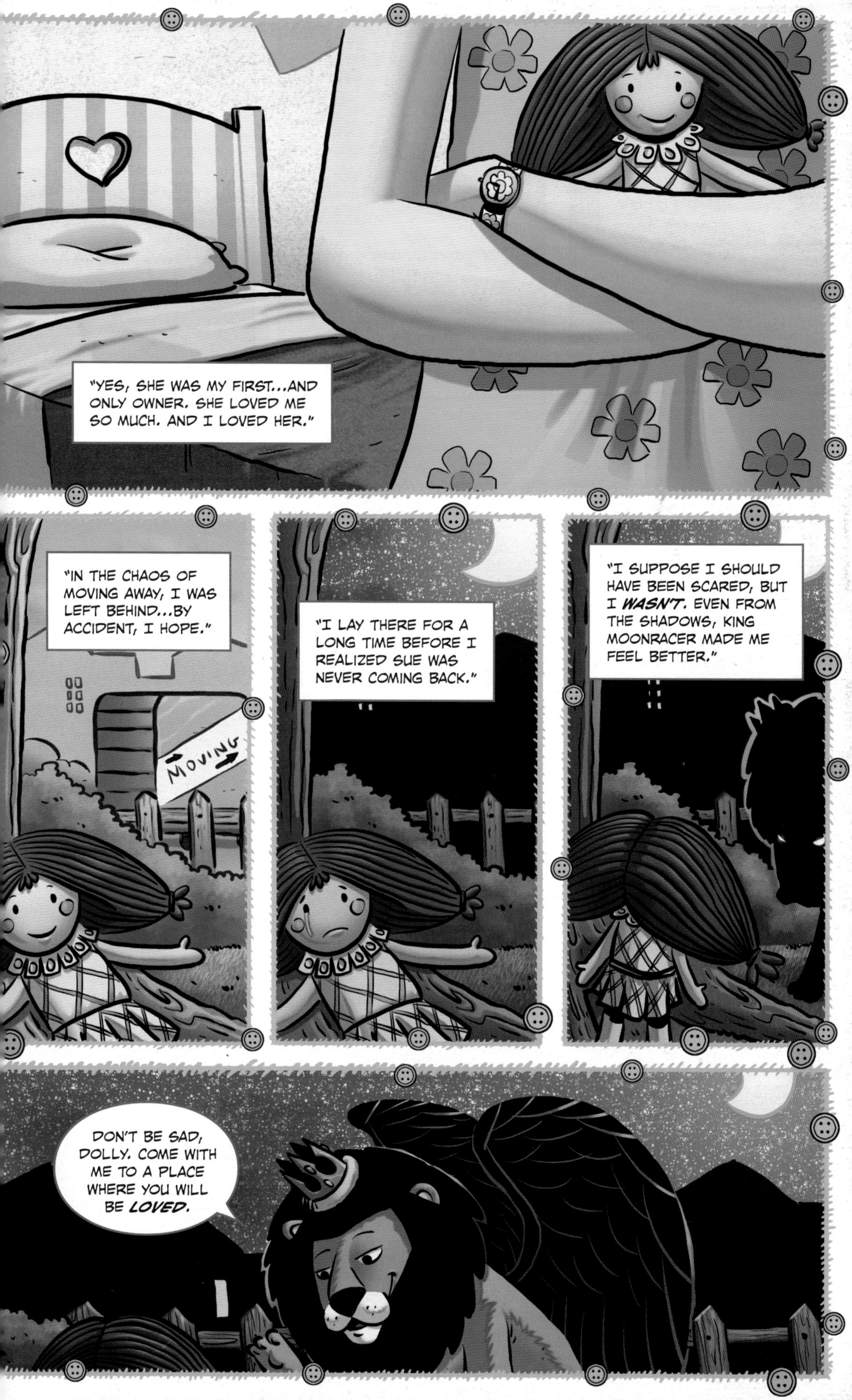
"YES, SHE WAS MY FIRST...AND ONLY OWNER. SHE LOVED ME SO MUCH. AND I LOVED HER."
"IN THE CHAOS OF MOVING AWAY, I WAS LEFT BEHIND...BY ACCIDENT, I HOPE."
MOVING
"I LAY THERE FOR A LONG TIME BEFORE I REALIZED SUE WAS NEVER COMING BACK."
"I SUPPOSE I SHOULD HAVE BEEN SCARED, BUT I *WASN'T*. EVEN FROM THE SHADOWS, KING MOONRACER MADE ME FEEL BETTER."
DON'T BE SAD, DOLLY. COME WITH ME TO A PLACE WHERE YOU WILL BE *LOVED*.

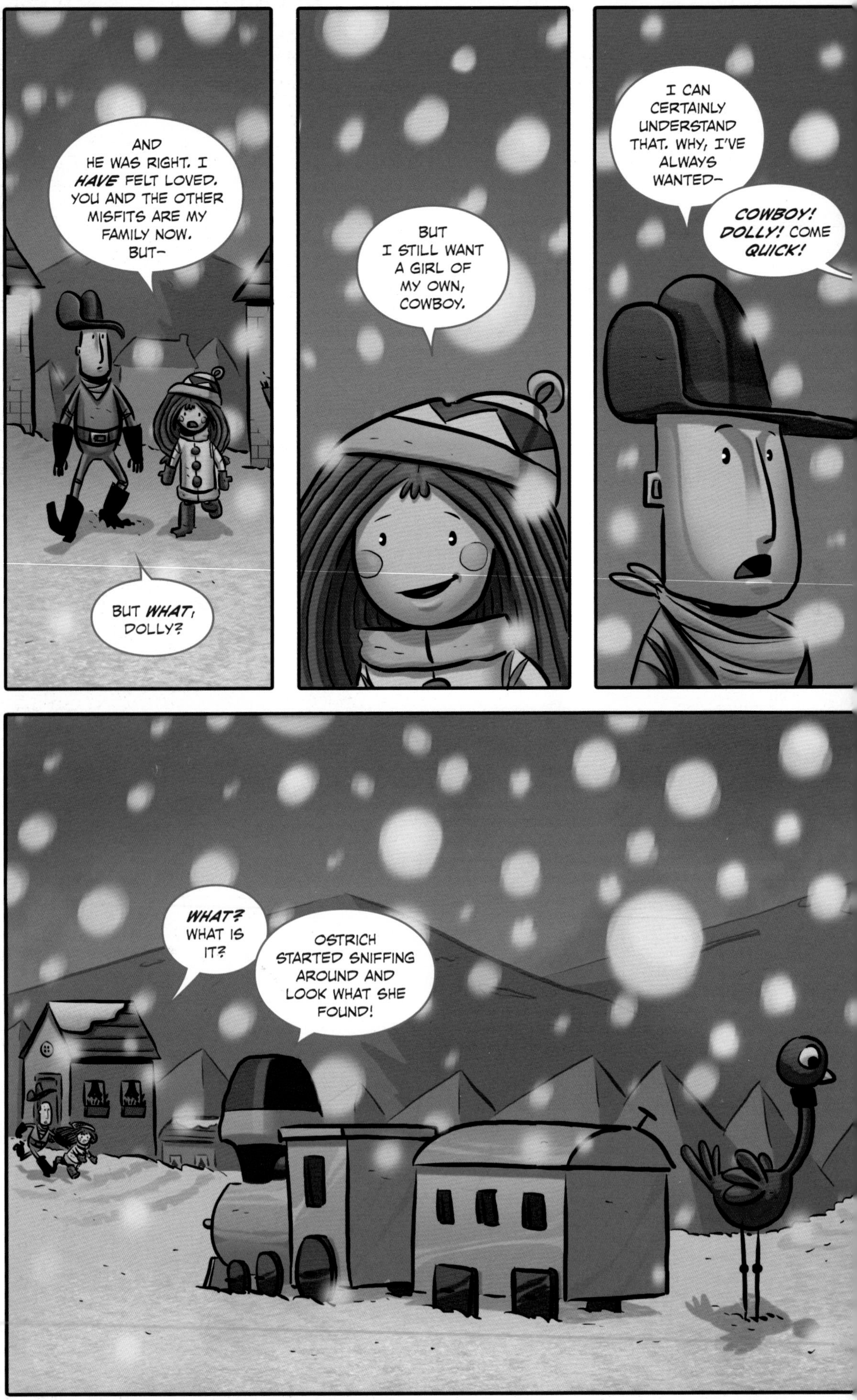
AND HE WAS RIGHT. I *HAVE* FELT LOVED. YOU AND THE OTHER MISFITS ARE MY FAMILY NOW. BUT–
BUT *WHAT*, DOLLY?
BUT I STILL WANT A GIRL OF MY OWN, COWBOY.
I CAN CERTAINLY UNDERSTAND THAT. WHY, I'VE ALWAYS WANTED–
COWBOY! DOLLY! COME *QUICK!*
WHAT? WHAT IS IT?
OSTRICH STARTED SNIFFING AROUND AND LOOK WHAT SHE FOUND!

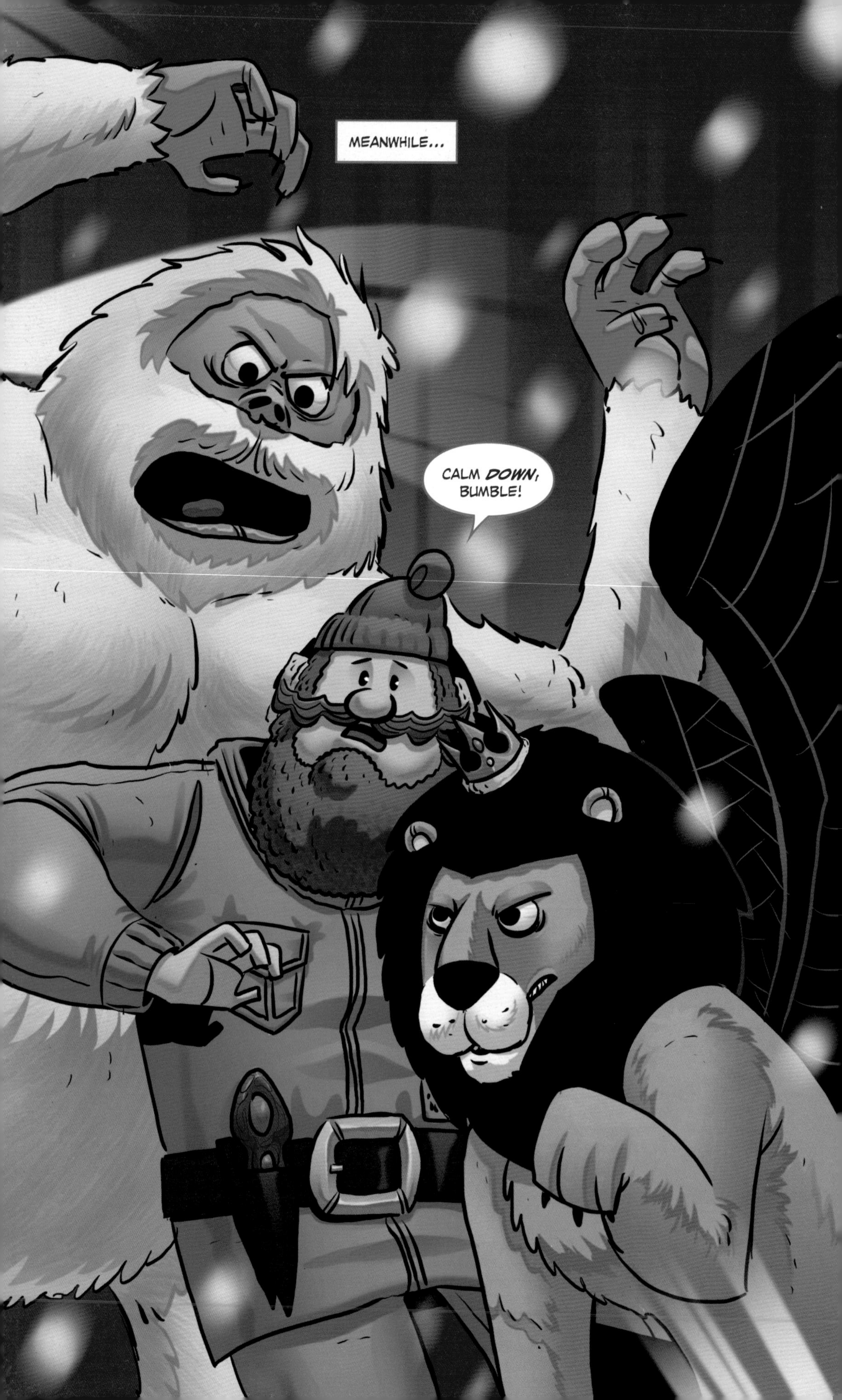
MEANWHILE...
CALM DOWN, BUMBLE!

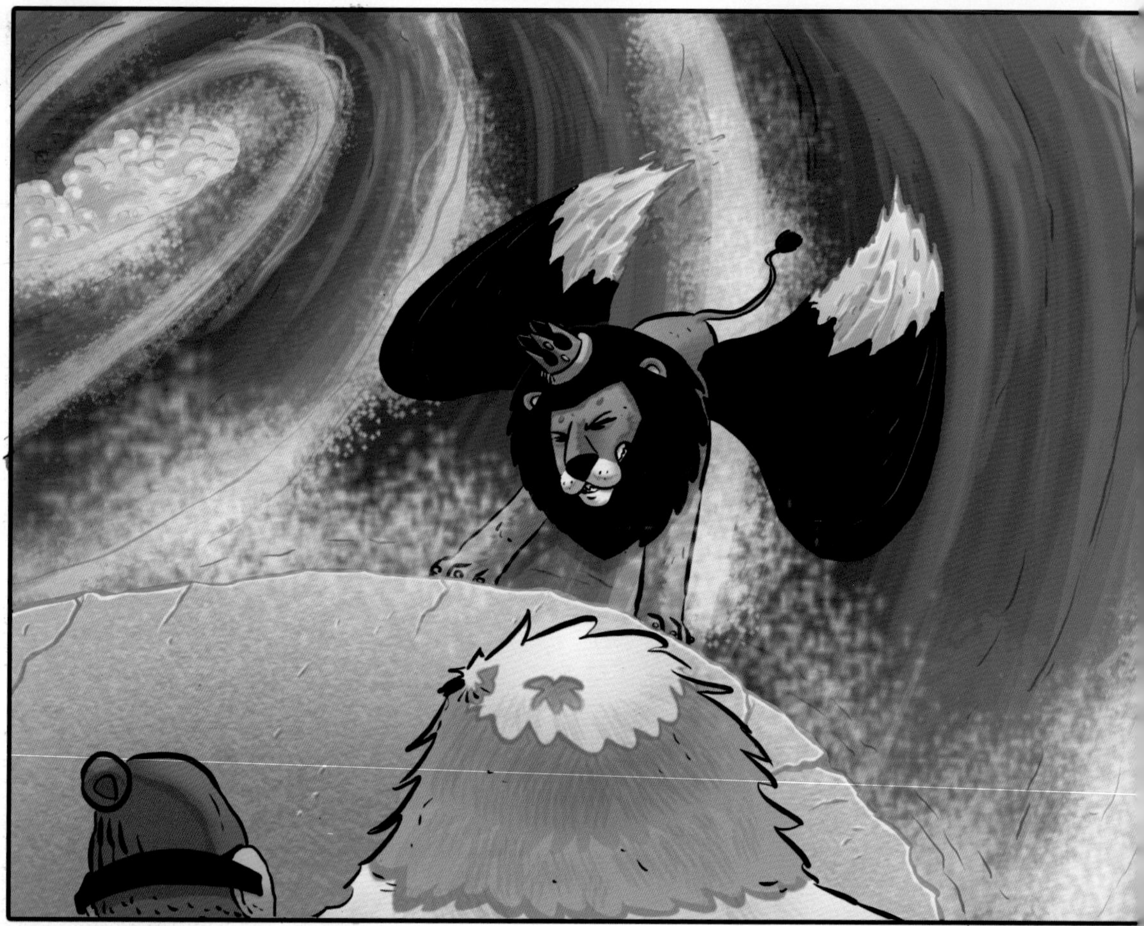

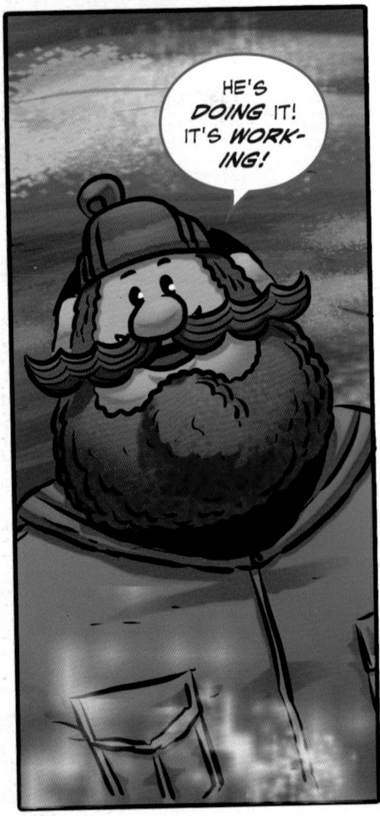
HE'S *DOING* IT! IT'S *WORK-ING!*

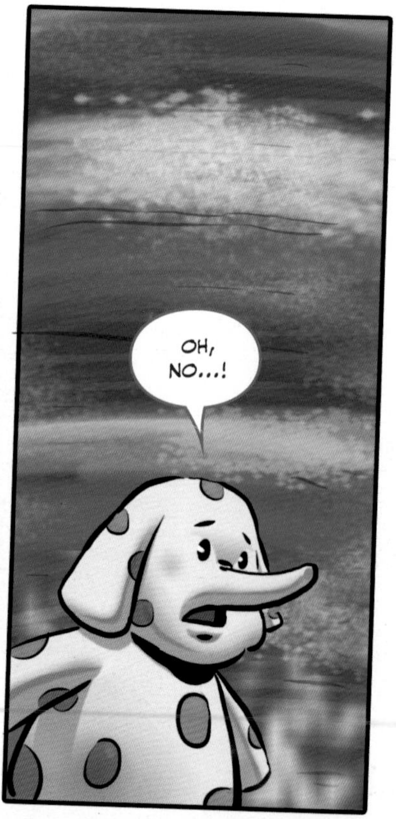
OH, NO...!

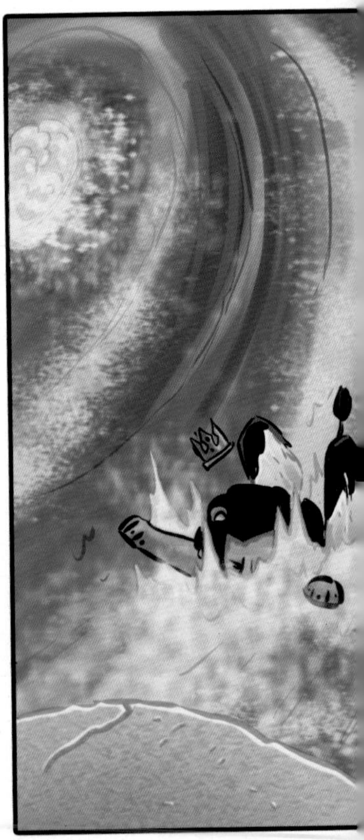

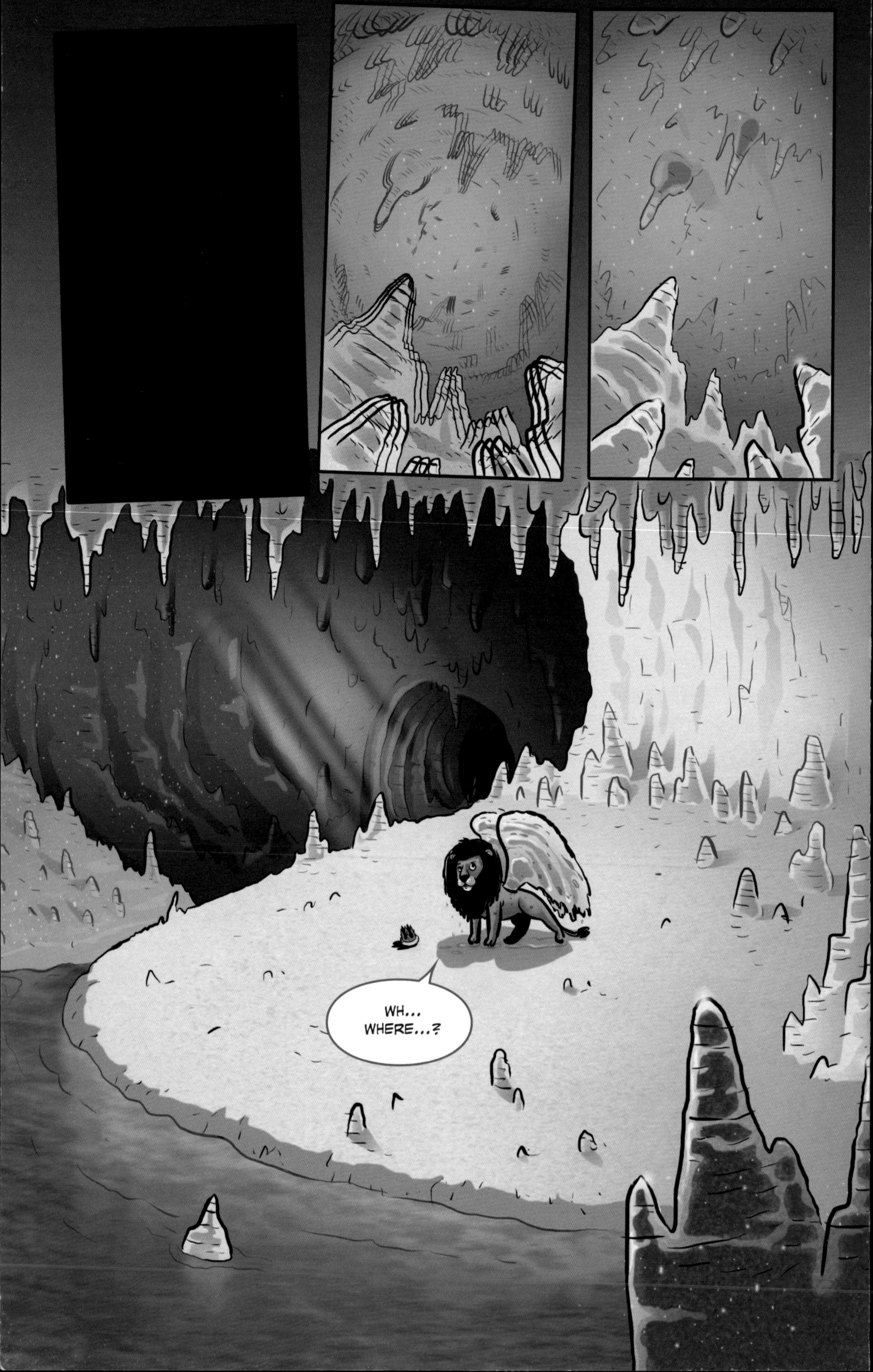
WH... WHERE...?

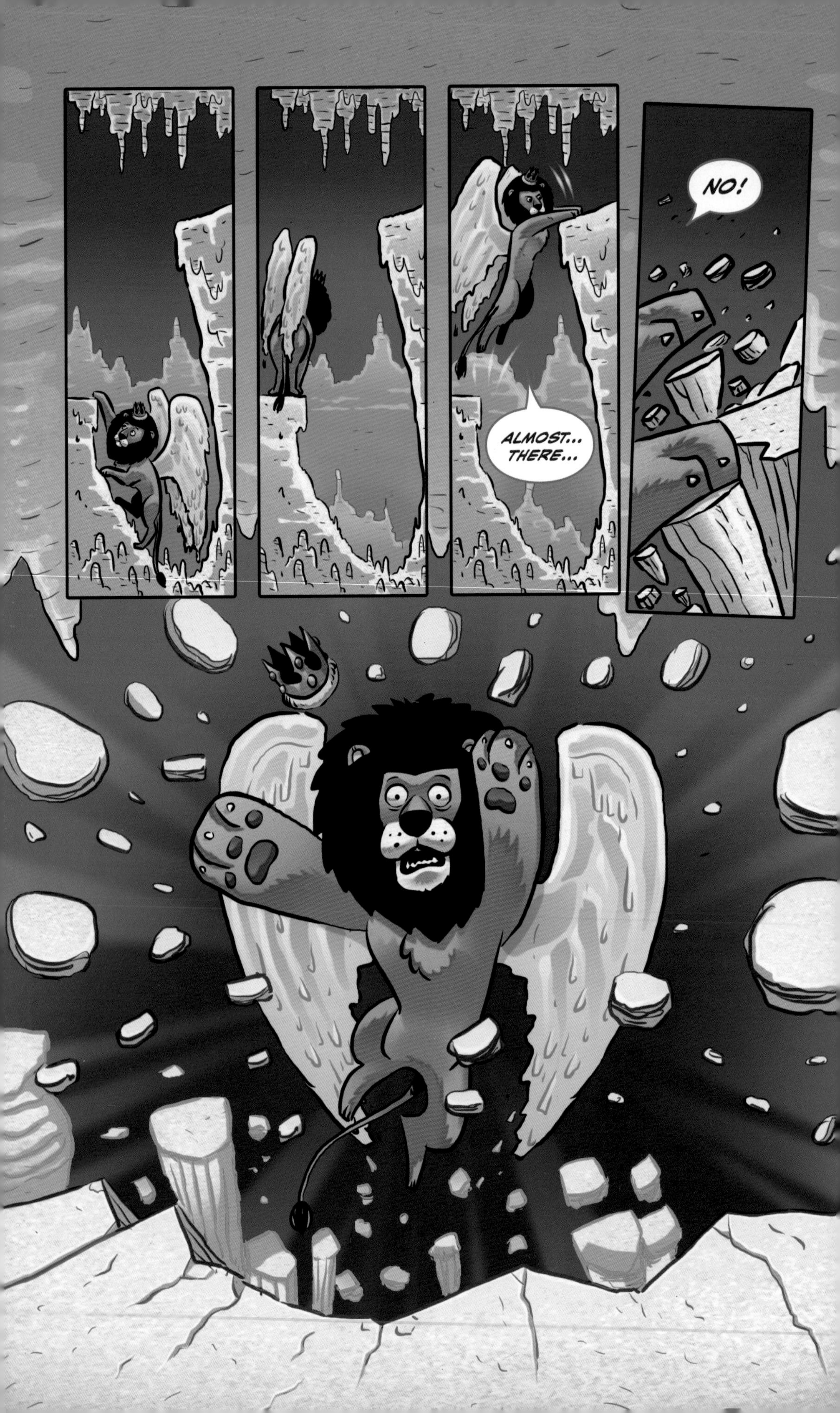
ALMOST... THERE...
NO!

CHAPTER FOUR

LOST AND FOUND

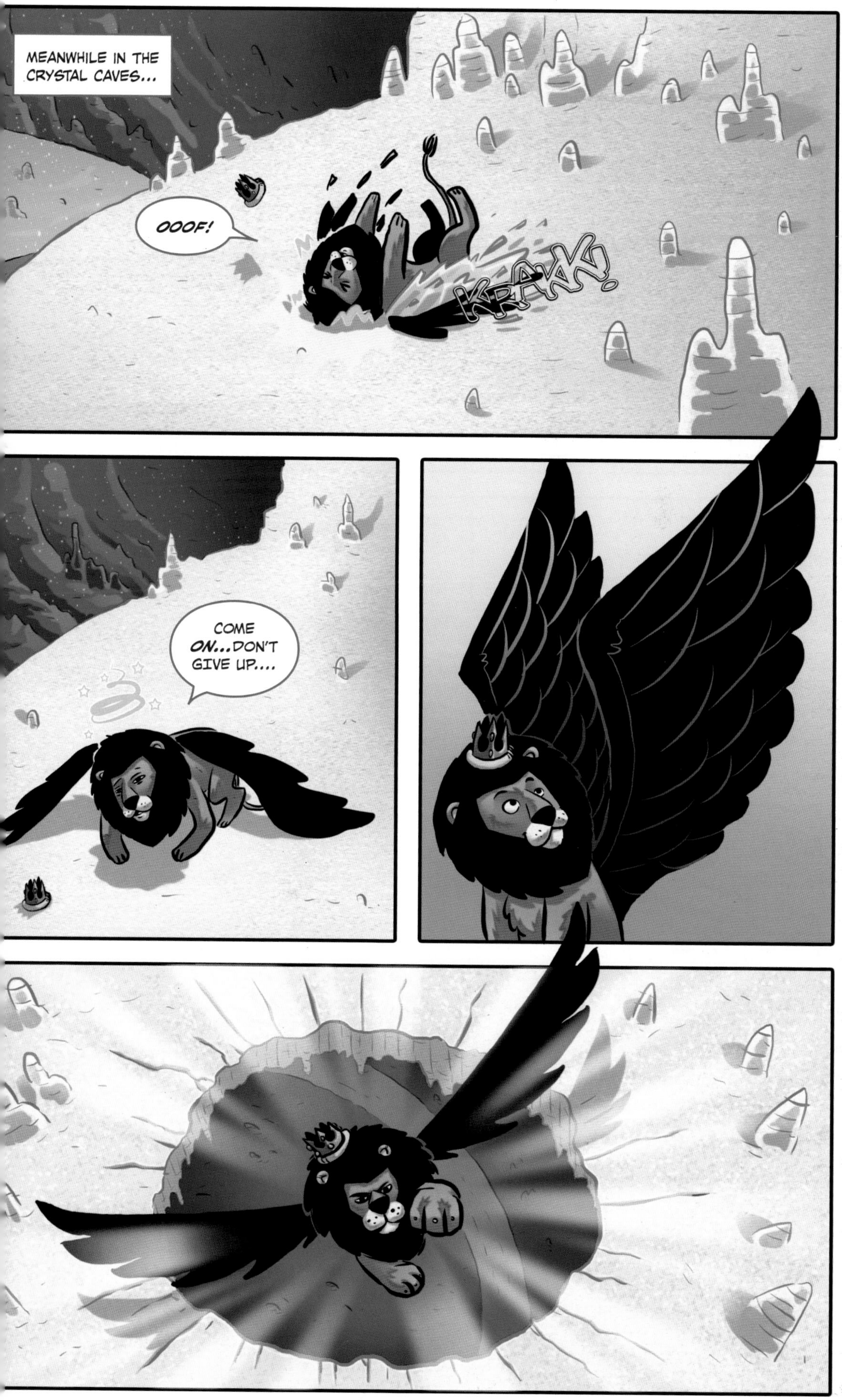
MEANWHILE IN THE CRYSTAL CAVES...
OOOF!
KRAKK!
COME ON...DON'T GIVE UP....

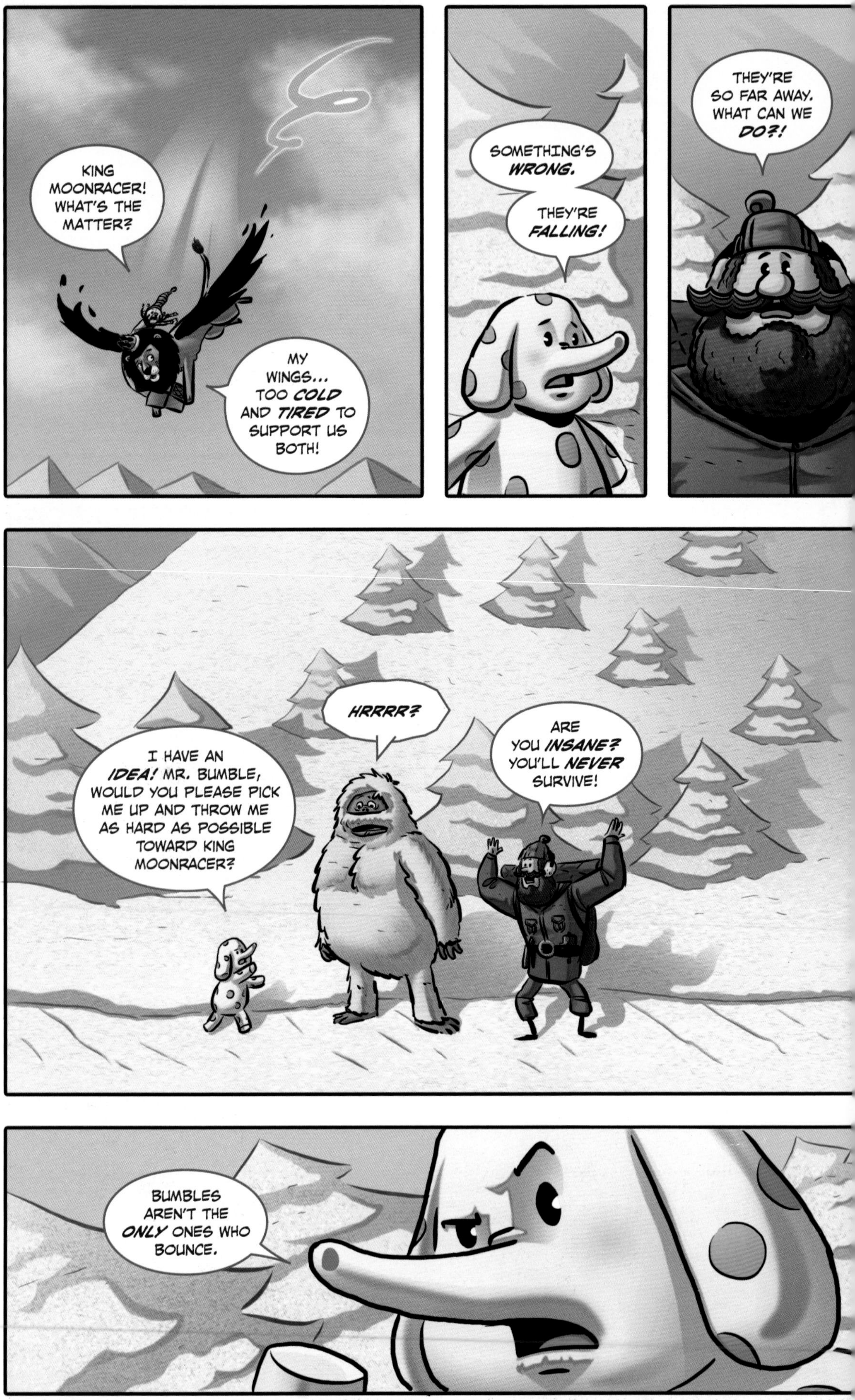
KING MOONRACER! WHAT'S THE MATTER?
MY WINGS... TOO COLD AND TIRED TO SUPPORT US BOTH!
SOMETHING'S WRONG.
THEY'RE FALLING!
THEY'RE SO FAR AWAY. WHAT CAN WE DO?!
I HAVE AN IDEA! MR. BUMBLE, WOULD YOU PLEASE PICK ME UP AND THROW ME AS HARD AS POSSIBLE TOWARD KING MOONRACER?
HRRRR?
ARE YOU INSANE? YOU'LL NEVER SURVIVE!
BUMBLES AREN'T THE ONLY ONES WHO BOUNCE.

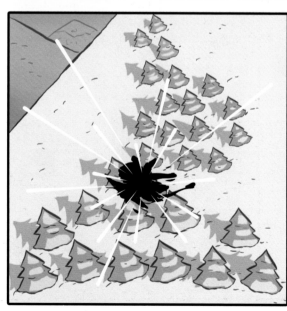

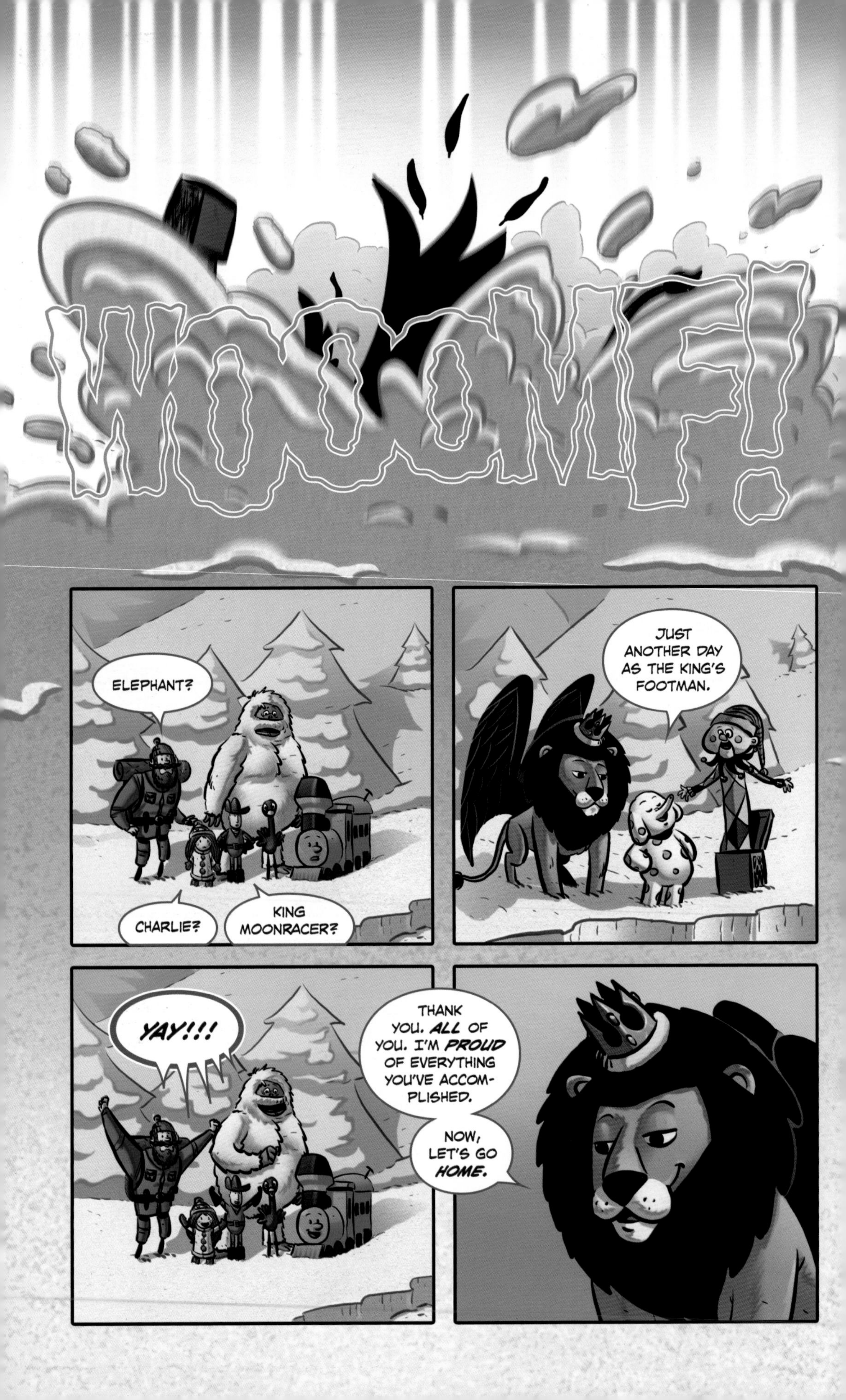
WOOOMF!
ELEPHANT?
CHARLIE?
KING MOONRACER?
JUST ANOTHER DAY AS THE KING'S FOOTMAN.
YAY!!!
THANK YOU. ALL OF YOU. I'M PROUD OF EVERYTHING YOU'VE ACCOMPLISHED.
NOW, LET'S GO HOME.

"A *RACE?!*"

DESPITE A *DIFFICULT* DAY OF CHALLENGES, THE EXHAUSTED TOYS WERE *HAPPIER* THAN EVER, HEADING HOME WITH THE HOPE THAT RUDOLPH WOULD KEEP HIS PROMISE. AND THAT SANTA WOULD FIND *HOMES* FOR EACH AND EVERY ONE OF THE MISFITS.

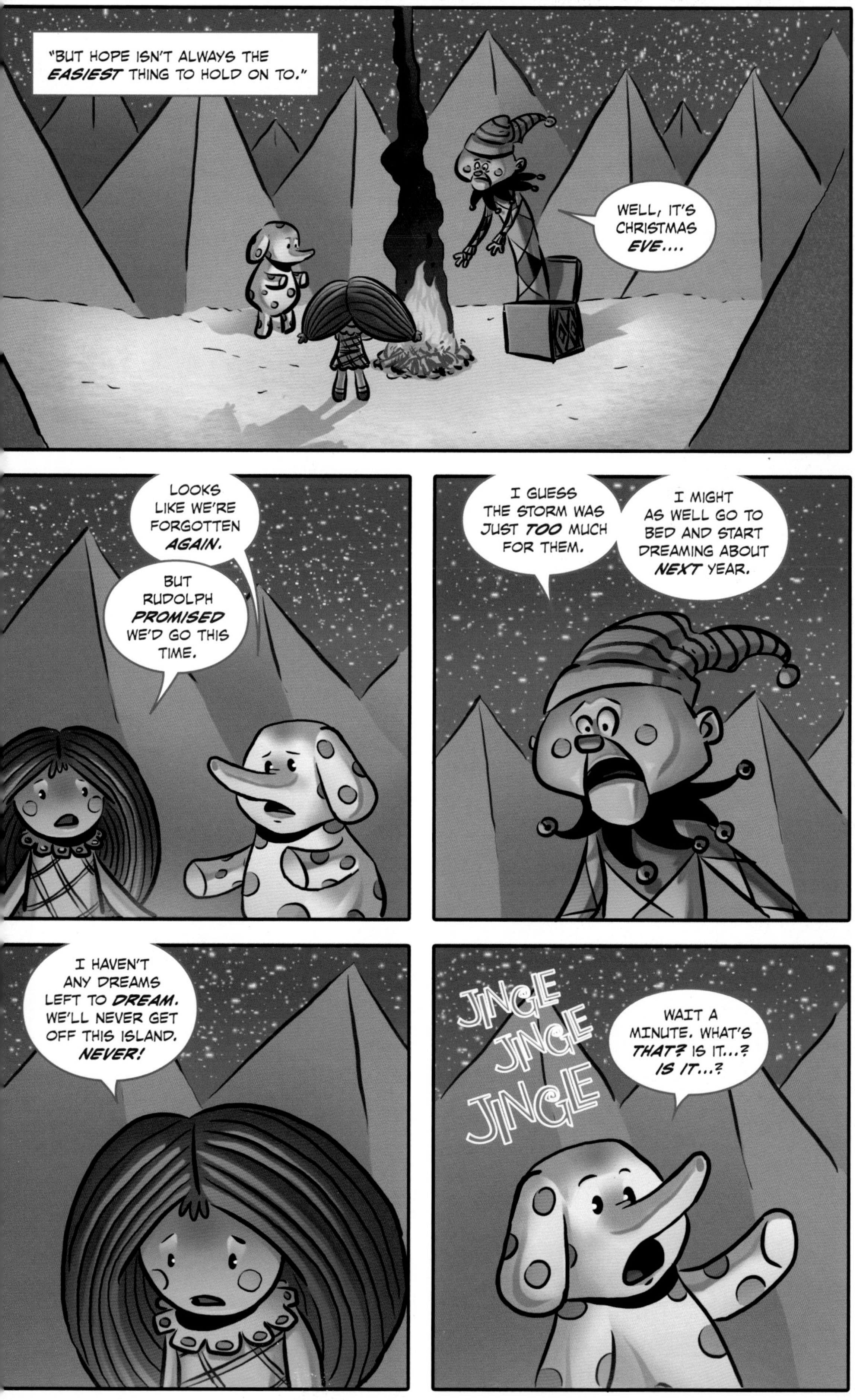
"BUT HOPE ISN'T ALWAYS THE EASIEST THING TO HOLD ON TO."
WELL, IT'S CHRISTMAS EVE....
LOOKS LIKE WE'RE FORGOTTEN AGAIN.
BUT RUDOLPH PROMISED WE'D GO THIS TIME.
I GUESS THE STORM WAS JUST TOO MUCH FOR THEM.
I MIGHT AS WELL GO TO BED AND START DREAMING ABOUT NEXT YEAR.
I HAVEN'T ANY DREAMS LEFT TO DREAM. WE'LL NEVER GET OFF THIS ISLAND. NEVER!
JINGLE JINGLE JINGLE
WAIT A MINUTE. WHAT'S THAT? IS IT...? IS IT...?

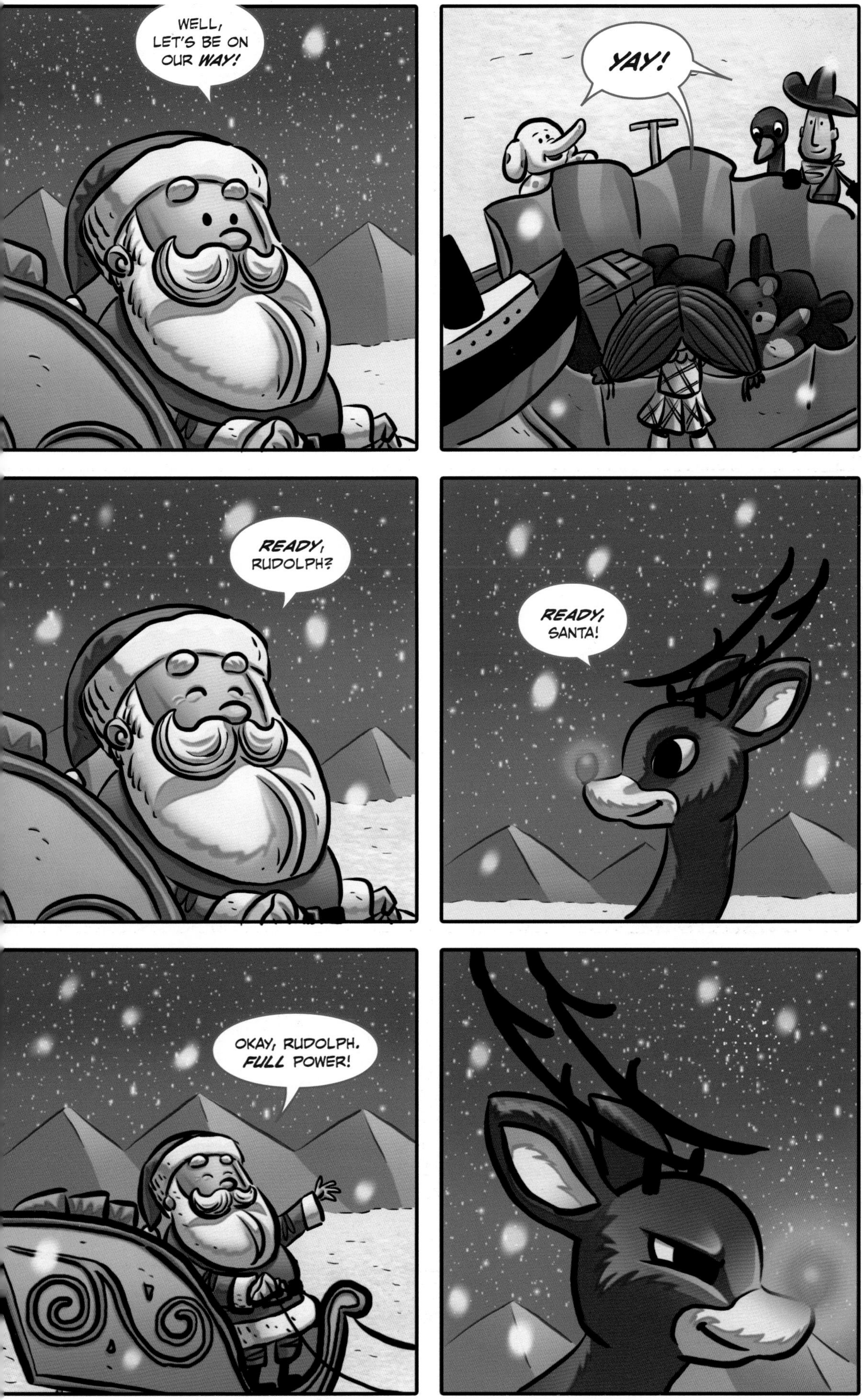
WELL, LET'S BE ON OUR *WAY!*
YAY!
READY, RUDOLPH?
READY, SANTA!
OKAY, RUDOLPH. *FULL* POWER!

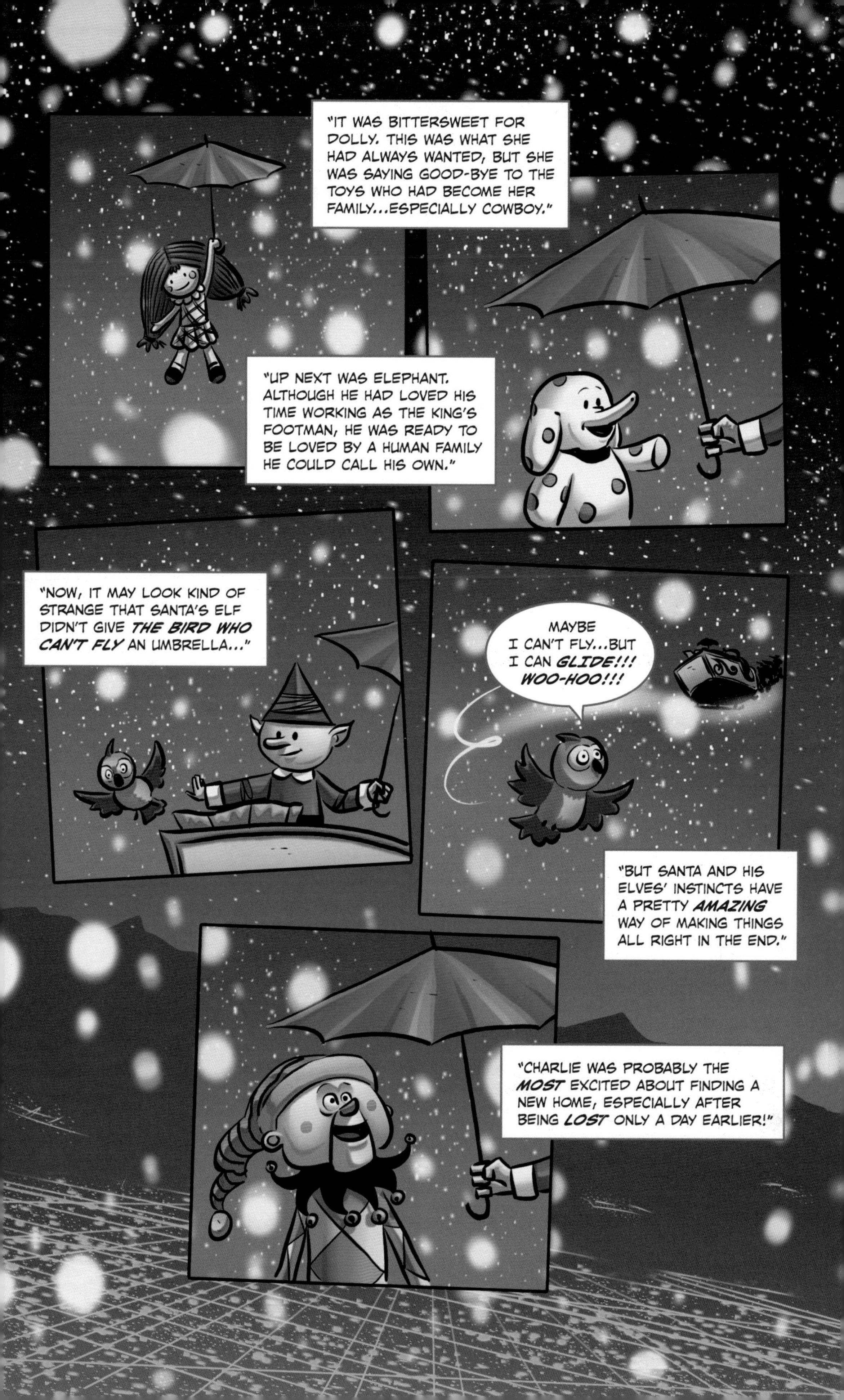
"IT WAS BITTERSWEET FOR DOLLY. THIS WAS WHAT SHE HAD ALWAYS WANTED, BUT SHE WAS SAYING GOOD-BYE TO THE TOYS WHO HAD BECOME HER FAMILY...ESPECIALLY COWBOY."
"UP NEXT WAS ELEPHANT. ALTHOUGH HE HAD LOVED HIS TIME WORKING AS THE KING'S FOOTMAN, HE WAS READY TO BE LOVED BY A HUMAN FAMILY HE COULD CALL HIS OWN."
"NOW, IT MAY LOOK KIND OF STRANGE THAT SANTA'S ELF DIDN'T GIVE *THE BIRD WHO CAN'T FLY* AN UMBRELLA..."
MAYBE I CAN'T FLY...BUT I CAN *GLIDE!!!* *WOO-HOO!!!*
"BUT SANTA AND HIS ELVES' INSTINCTS HAVE A PRETTY *AMAZING* WAY OF MAKING THINGS ALL RIGHT IN THE END."
"CHARLIE WAS PROBABLY THE *MOST* EXCITED ABOUT FINDING A NEW HOME, ESPECIALLY AFTER BEING *LOST* ONLY A DAY EARLIER!"

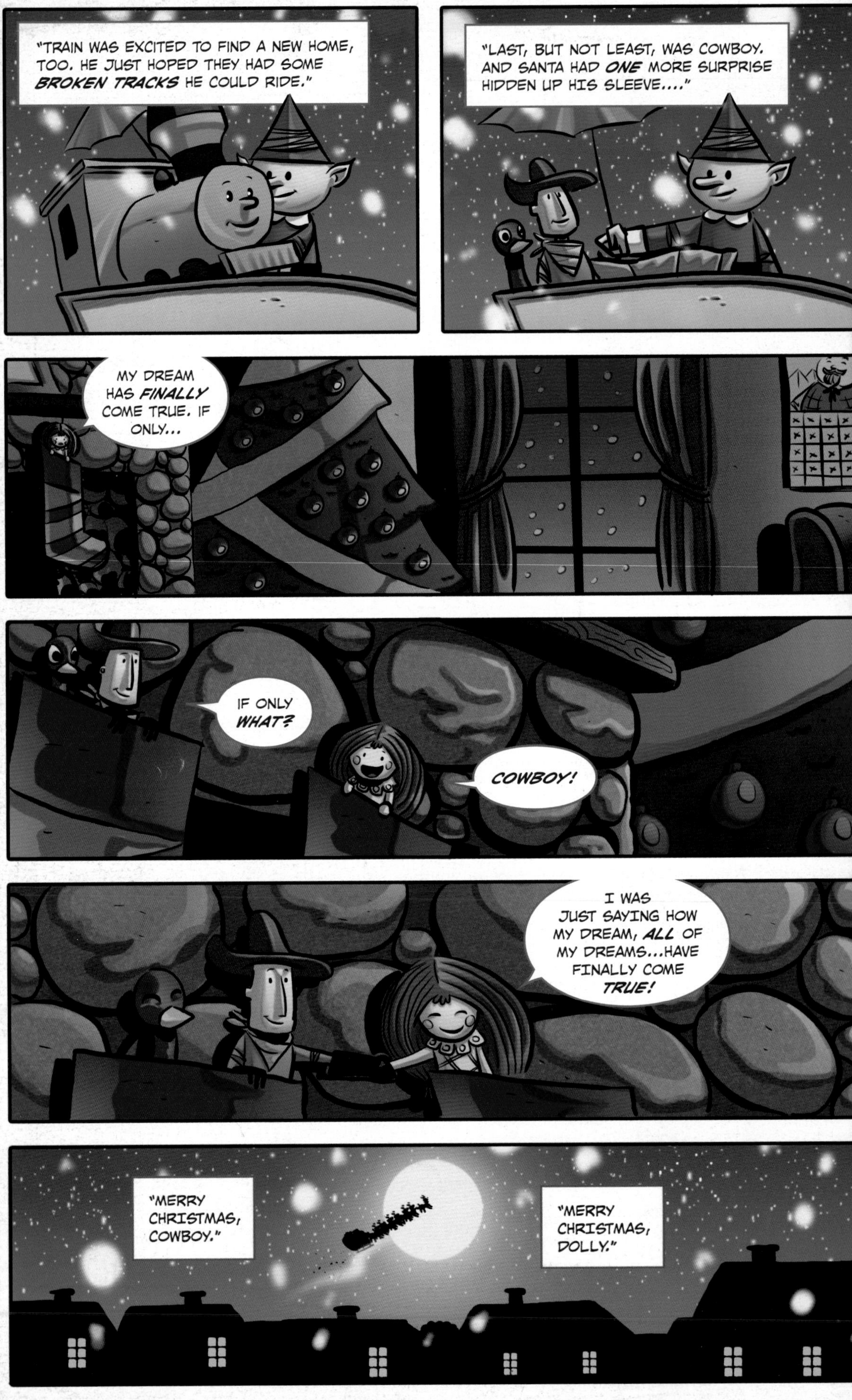
"TRAIN WAS EXCITED TO FIND A NEW HOME, TOO. HE JUST HOPED THEY HAD SOME BROKEN TRACKS HE COULD RIDE."
"LAST, BUT NOT LEAST, WAS COWBOY. AND SANTA HAD ONE MORE SURPRISE HIDDEN UP HIS SLEEVE...."
MY DREAM HAS FINALLY COME TRUE. IF ONLY...
IF ONLY WHAT?
COWBOY!
I WAS JUST SAYING HOW MY DREAM, ALL OF MY DREAMS...HAVE FINALLY COME TRUE!
"MERRY CHRISTMAS, COWBOY."
"MERRY CHRISTMAS, DOLLY."

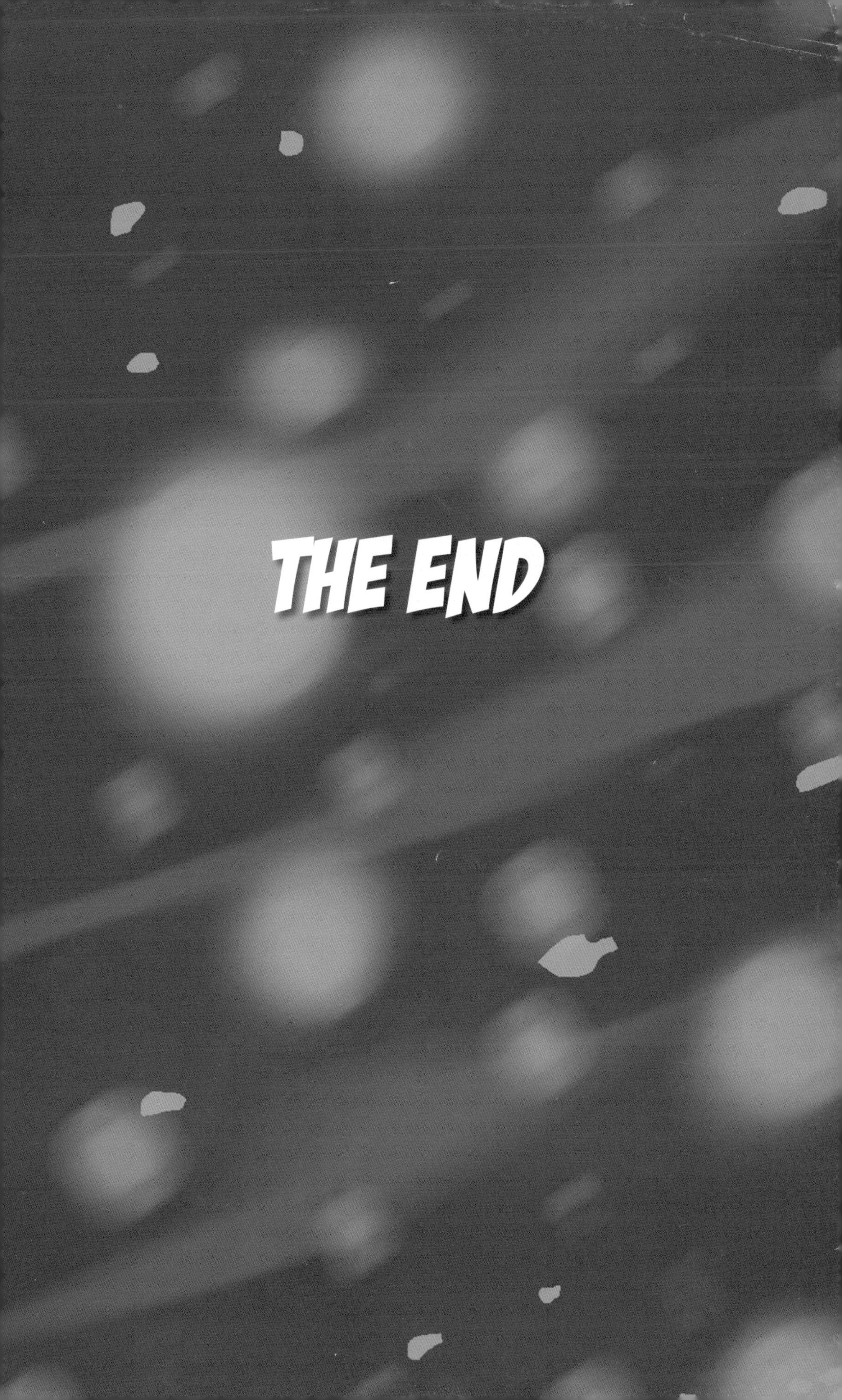
THE END

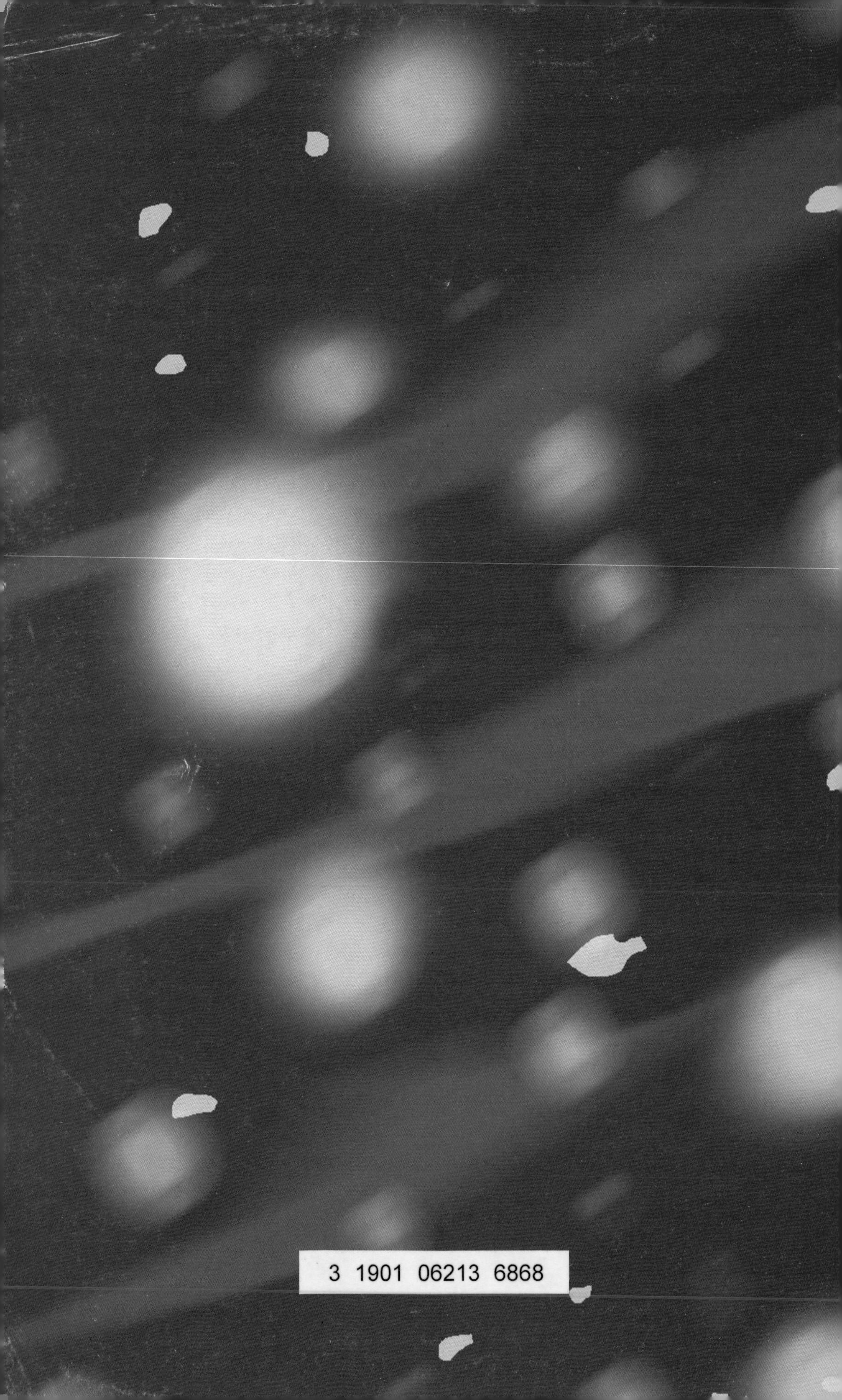